LIGHTNING STRIKES TWICE

Lacey Dancer

A KISMET® Romance

METEOR PUBLISHING CORPORATION
Bensalem, Pennsylvania

For Kate. You gave me Stryker McGuire and he spawned Slater, Sloane and Mike. So this one is for you. Thanks.

LACEY DANCER

Lacey Dancer is a dream weaver. Her age is according to the day and the problems belonging to that moment. Her goals are to give to others the best of herself and to her work more than she did the day before. Her life is mated with one man's, for now a quarter of a century of loving. From that love came two children who alternately make her proud and drive her nuts. But that's living and loving by the choices she has made.

Other books by Lacey Dancer:

PROLOGUE

The air swooshed by her face, whispers of flight
without manmade power. The wide wings of the
brightly colored kite over her head lifted her on the
thermals to sweep her in graceful arcs across the blue
sky. Tempest hung suspended from the hang-glider
harness, lips parted at the challenge of pitting herself
against a force stronger than she, in the joy of the
moment and the feeling of total freedom that filled
her. Here she was mistress of the world below, commanded only by the air currents and the skill of her
own hands. No human voice intruded, smothering,
caring, demanding in the so kind ways that she be
someone else, that she do something with her life,
that she live up to her potential. Behind the protective goggles, her eyes sparkled with irrepressible joie
de vivre, a death wish some said, a need to be outrageous pronounced others, and finally, most agreed,
a need to shock. She denied nothing, for she had

neither the answers to the restlessness that made settling into one mold impossible nor the desire to become a practicing member of the Whitney-King
dynasty that controlled so much wealth and power
both stateside and internationally.

She was Tempest. Pure energy. Always on the go.
Always reaching for the stars, often tumbling tail
over teakettle in an attempt to go where no woman
had gone before. Dare anything, try anything once.
Never say quit. No fear. No need to be anyone but
herself. She smiled, her lips a wicked curve in a face
that, in repose, was pretty and, in the thrill of moments
like this, so alive that no man, woman, or child could
deny the pull of her beauty. Her eyes were the clear
blue of a sky at noon. Her lips were full, a perfect
bow that invited a man's kiss and seldom delivered,
for their owner had been caught, burned so completely
in desire's trap that she allowed her passion only one
outlet now, pure freedom. Freedom to go, to race the
storm, to ride the whim of the moment, to soar on the
promise of danger and excitement.

Suddenly, the air around her changed. The sun
slipped behind a cloud. The scent of rain clung to
the breeze. Her smile should have gone into hiding
as the atmosphere started to shimmer and hiss. It
didn't. It widened, adrenaline pouring into her veins
at the new challenge Mother Nature was flinging at
her. Her fingers, long and elegant, the kind to pour
tea or soothe a fractious child, tightened on the bar
in front of her. More alert than before, her body
swayed easily with the quickening breeze. Her head
lifted, her eyes flashing with delight and the acceptance of the elemental gauntlet thrown at her slender

body. The first drops of rain hit as she scanned the trees dotting the landscape below. The sky darkened, demanding her attention but getting only a little of the precious commodity that stood between her and the losing of this silent battle. The glider swooped lower, the wind whistling now, warning Tempest that she was alone, at its mercy, caught between heaven and earth in its grip. It tugged at the one-piece suit she wore, stabbing invisible fingers against her skin, and tried, with its increasing moan, to make her cry quits. She laughed in its face, her gaze riveted on the minuscule clearing that she had chosen as her landing spot.

Nature responded, clearly angry that a frail piece of humanity would have so little respect for its power. The kite dipped down, its wings swaying as Tempest demanded its obedience to her will. The trees rushed up, perhaps obeying the command of the angry wind and the insulted elements. Suddenly, sensing its loss looming so imminently on the horizon, Mother Nature lifted its hand to punish the foolish transgressor. Scooped up by the air currents, Tempest missed the clearing and slammed into the top of a tree. The kite caught the limbs, at the last moment becoming the savior instead of the servant of the slender woman who had commanded it. Tempest hit the trunk, hard enough to knock her unconscious in spite of the protective helmet she wore. She hung limp from the harness as the clouds wept over her.

Stryker McGuire maneuvered the rental car over the unpaved path to the hang glide launch area that Tempest had shown him two days before. If he had been a man who ever allowed his temper to master him, he would have been cursing every pothole and the woman who had slipped from his bed and his arms to disobey him directly in this latest of her death wish escapades. It didn't help that the weather report he had just heard on the radio promised rain, scattered showers, some heavy. The moisture that fell on the windshield was enough evidence. If Tempest had been another woman, he would have said she had heard about the promised precipitation and changed her mind about going up. But not Tempest Whitney-King. For six years he had been her watch-dog of sorts, courtesy of her father, who was his employer. It was he who had gone to Paris to convince the police that she hadn't meant to insult their ancestry, but rather her French was haphazard. The man had accepted the explanation, knowing full well it was a lie. But one did not antagonize the Whitney-Kings of this world. Then there had been the young Austrian count who had chased her unmercifully for the benefit of every tabloid in the world and the utter, complete embarrassment of her conventional family. His diplomatic skills had been stretched to the limit to extricate her from that amorous mess. The count was now married and the father of two, thank God. Then there had been that time in Cairo and the camel race. Athens and the mistreated goat. Buenos Aires and the lost passport. The Bahamas and the boat race with its ringer driver, Tempest. The cross-country car race in Baja and the illegal alien. The white water rafting incident that had left her in the hospital with a broken arm surrounded by a horde of family members grateful for the life of a little girl she had rescued. His career, his nightmares, his dreams were peppered with her exploits. He had gray hairs already, one he was positive for every damn thing she had pulled since her fifteenth birthday. Her family loved her, God only knew how. Her smile was the kind that a man could die for if he didn't kill her first. Her body, when she wasn't busy trying to break a bone or two, was made for loving, his loving.

He jerked the car to a stop beside her truck and scanned the area, his eyes narrowed for better visibility through the rain. No Tempest. Binoculars in hand, he searched the sky, not even realizing he had left the shelter of the vehicle so that he would not miss an inch of the angry heavens. No Tempest. Worry drew new lines in his face, increasing the strength and the purpose that sat so easily on the clearly defined features. His eyes were as dark as midnight, deeper, more secretive. Cupping his hands to his mouth, he called her name. Silence. No Tempest. He turned in a semicircle, his search now for a vantage point. If she wasn't in the air or here, then she was down somewhere. A tall pine stood about three hundred yards away. Long strides ate up the distance. Sure hands and feet carried him aloft, over the tops of the shorter trees, high enough to scan the hills and the valley below the promontory. Suddenly, he froze in his visual sweeps of the area. A tiny splash of scarlet and vivid yellow a couple of miles away caught his eye—her favorite colors suspended about a third of the way down a tree much like his own. His face tightened as he retraced his path to the ground. The truck with the ropes and extra equipment it contained screamed out of the clearing, its tires complaining at the lack of traction. He neither noticed nor cared. He couldn't be sure, but he thought he had seen a body hanging limply from the harness of the kite.

His mind on the terrain, his heart with the woman who had shared the hours of the night with him for the last week, he fought the vehicle and the elements to reach her, to bring her warmth in the cold of the rain, shelter in the face of the attack by nature, and safety as she dangled precariously between earth and sky.

"Tempest." The only word Stryker spoke. Her name. His curse.

Finally, he reached the clearing that lay at the base of the tree. He slued to a halt and jumped from the truck. She was there, hung like a discarded doll, unmoving, her beautiful blue eyes closed, her silky red hair caged in the scarlet helmet that he prayed had saved her from serious injury. For one instant he stared at her motionless figure, every sense, every reaction frozen by the terror of the very real possibility that she no longer lived. For the first time in his life he knew the feeling of total, irrational fear, fear that couldn't be suppressed or even endured. Sweat broke out on his face, washed away by the rain the moment it appeared. It was a physical exertion to force himself to move and an even more demanding effort to slam the lid on his fear and concentrate solely on getting aloft. He moved swiftly, rigging himself to ropes and harness. Climbing the tree was no problem. Getting Tempest down alone without hurting her would be. Stryker wove his way through the branches, every handhold bringing him closer.

Her first moan was one of the most wonderful sounds he had ever heard. He exhaled deeply, climbing faster now as her groans came more frequently, growing in strength as she returned to consciousness. Now, there was a different kind of danger.

"Tempest, don't move," Stryker ordered in a hard voice as he saw her hands clench. Five more feet and he could touch her. Five more minutes and he'd have her secure if not down. "Stay still or so help me I'll wring your neck," he added for good measure.

Tempest shifted groggily, her lashes fluttering at the sound of his voice. Worry threaded the dark sound. She attempted a smile to reassure him, but nothing was working quite right at the moment. She tried her voice, needing to reach him. "Stryker?"

"Stay still," he roared.

As her senses began to clear, perhaps jammed out of the fog by Stryker's rough tone, she realized the seriousness of her position. Her lashes blinked twice as she was finally able to focus on the face she knew in so many moods, the body she had touched in passion and anger, the voice that could tame the wildness in her soul for long moments, a feat no other being on the face of the earth had ever done. "Don't shout. I'm not deaf."

Stryker reached her, flipped a rope around the tree to secure his position. "Damn fool. I told you not to do this alone." His words were rough, angry; his hands gentle, competent. He stared into her eyes through the protective visor of the helmet. She looked half awake but the pupils were reacting correctly to the bright flashes of lightning. His breath came out in an audible rush of relief that he didn't notice as he completed checking her for broken bones.

"I'm sorry I messed up again but I couldn't resist." Tempest touched his cheek gently, needing to wipe away the fear that she could see in his eyes. Stryker angry was a price she could afford for her mishaps. Stryker afraid hurt her in ways she couldn't explain.

"I couldn't resist. The sun was shining and I had to fly," she said softly, ignoring the wind and the rain that were swiping at their precarious position. She wanted to share the joy of her experience with him in ways she hadn't tried since she was a naive child with a thirst for all the delights the world had to offer but with no one who could share, understand, or sympathize with her need to savor everything creation had to give. "It was beautiful, free. You should have come," she finished simply, her fingers tracing his tight lips.

Her words, her touch. So damn gentle yet a knife to slash his heart with fear, his mind with emotions he couldn't control, and his body with the memories of passion and dark whispers of need. He fought every reaction. He wasn't ready to face what she meant to him and what this stunt had done to the fragile relationship that had ambushed them both and been born in the still of the night and her innocence and his unrelenting desire.

"I asked you to wait until the weather settled down," he growled harshly, denying his feelings and her tenderness. He eased her from the last of the harness, holding her body to his in a lovers' embrace. There was nothing of the lover in his expression or his eyes as he stared into her rapt face and tried to forget the sight of her hanging motionless from the fragile ropes that had probably saved her life. He was used to anger when he was near her. Her hell-for-leather attitude made that emotional state a given. But until today, he had never experienced rage, pure, untainted with any kind of restraint or reason. He looked into her eyes, seeing not one hint of remorse or even any real idea of the danger she had been in, and knew that on the day he drew his last breath he wouldn't forget this moment.

"You're determined to kill yourself." He glared at her, hardly noticing that a capricious shift in the wind sent the kite tumbling to the ground. He had her. That was all he would allow himself to acknowledge. That and fury at her crazy dice game with death. Suddenly an emotional cork popped from the bottled up feelings that had been suppressed for so long. "For six years I've tried to keep you safe, out of trouble. I've watched you grow up, prayed you'd find yourself. Seven days ago you gave yourself to me. I thought I mattered, but in the end, this end, I see that I was only fooling myself." Even as he ended their relationship with words he was binding her to him for the descent. "But no more. I won't tie myself to a woman who cares so little for those who love her that she constantly risks herself needlessly. I won't share the night with you, knowing that at any moment you may slip from my arms and skip out to dance on a whim, throw yourself from a cliff because it's there, or just move on because this place, this time, doesn't suit you for some reason even you don't understand."

Tempest heard the words, focused on them, hearing his pain echoing through all those who had loved her and cried out in the same kind of tormented voices. She wanted to be what they wanted her to be. She had tried and failed so many times that she had finally realized to make one more attempt was to kill herself in ways that had nothing to do with physical death. She faced him, the passion that would always hold him in her memory, the caring he gave with every breath he drew. Always, unless she set him free, he would be caught in the cage of that caring, that fear that still lurked in his dark eyes. Because she knew the pain of imprisonment, its slow death, she looked this challenge in the eye and gathered her courage to play this game to the last drop of her nerve.

"I'm sorry," she whispered, tears she wouldn't have shed for herself quivering on the tips of her lashes. He didn't notice and the rain was quick to hide the weakness, perhaps atoning for the attempt it had made on her life.

"Damn you, Tempest. I held you last night. We talked about this flight. I told you that the weather looked iffy. I even offered to come with you when it cleared. Fool that I am I didn't think to demand your word," he said bitterly.

Tempest absorbed each word as a blow to her already hurting body. She didn't fight him, not physically, for he was taking her down, his every movement smooth, strong, and sure.

"I'll see you out of this. I'll even come if you

call or your father sends me. But, as of now, I plan to forget I ever held you, ever believed you cared for me.'' His feet touched the earth. He held her in front of him, scanning her eyes through the helmet visor he hadn't removed. "Do you understand me?"

"Yes." She remembered the warmth of his arms, the times he had tried to understand her. He had given so much and she so little. He thought she didn't care. He was wrong. "You're right. I thought I could lose myself in you but it wasn't enough." She watched the fire in his eyes grow cold. She felt that cold to her bones. She smiled, the one gesture so perfect that only a man at the end of his rope would have been fooled. "Thank you for saving my skin. All those times before and this one, too."

Stryker searched her eyes, seeking the key to this strange, quixotic woman who could melt his natural caution with a look, who drew more response with a light brush of her body than the most practiced of bedmates. She had taught him fear, rage, and a host of other uncomfortable reactions that he could have cheerfully lived without. He had wanted her from the first moment he had seen her, all long legs, carrot hair, and camellia skin. She had been fifteen at the time, belligerent, sure that he wouldn't believe her about the scrape that had caused her father to send his newest fair-haired boy to the rescue. He had believed her, against all evidence, he had looked into the honesty of those blue eyes and seen something that her family had seemed to miss. Integrity and honor. Heart. From that moment on, he had watched over her, his part-time job with his other duties for Whitney-King International and his avocation, for he felt drawn to the woman emerging painfully from a rocky adolescent. She was a fighter, his Tempest. Only in his thoughts had he ever called her that. She fought for life, for those with less than she, for ideas that others found uncomfortable, and for freedom, hers. Without realizing it, Stryker lifted his fingers and traced her lips. Six long years of waiting for her to grow up, hoping that she would one day look at him and see more than the man who took her side against the world. He had thought he had her trust. And he had discovered the lie, her first and for him the most devastating of all. When he had awakened this morning and found himself alone, he had known where she would be. He had prayed he was wrong, even gone through the motions of seeking her in the room and later downstairs before coming after her.

"It could have been so good for us," he murmured, almost gently. The thought of never having the right to hold her close to his heart, to hear her wild cries of release, to see that devil take the hindmost smile was a knife in his gut.

Tempest stood still, agony at the calm, almost dispassionate delivery of his words so intense that she couldn't have moved even to save herself from hearing more.

"I believed in you. You've never lied to me even by omission. I trusted you."

She could have told him then. But in that moment, she took a giant, painful step toward maturity. He had given her passion, taught her of her body, her depth of loving, and her need. He had shown her, too, his own vulnerability. He would always look to see where he put his foot, to reach high, but he would always know where the safety net was and who held it. He was the problem solver and she was the problem with no solution.

"I had to go." That was the truth but not the whole.

He closed his eyes, his fingers leaving the warmth of the lips he had possessed and the mouth that had profaned his trust.

Tempest wiggled for release.

Stryker opened his eyes, all traces of his anguish erased as though it had never been. His gaze was analytical, clinical, detached. His hands supported but offered nothing personal. "You're going to the hospital."

Tempest accepted the command, anything to satisfy him and free them both from the hell that couldn't be changed. "All right."

He looked at her suspiciously but she didn't see. Her eyes were on the kite and its ripped scarlet wings. The strips of bright fabric were slender streams of blood against the trees. Fitting. She had set out to celebrate life and ended by embracing a death she hadn't expected.

ONE

"Josh should have been here but the office called with a problem. We probably won't see him until dinner," Pippa explained as she handed Stryker a glass of iced tea.

He took a sip and leaned back in his chair, relaxing completely with a deep sigh. It had been a long year, one crisis after another. "I didn't expect to be entertained when you invited me to lay over here on my way to the Bahamas."

"Not entertained. I don't think you entertain friends." She grinned and drank from her own glass. She had liked this man from the first moment she had met him. She enjoyed males who faced the world with courage, intelligence, and a light hand with their strength. Finesse and subtlety had always intrigued her and Stryker had a great deal of both. "How did you find your brother and Joy?"

"The doctor has given Slater a clean bill of health,

although he's still not completely back to normal. He's got some physical therapy to finish and he's supposed to take it easy getting back to a full work load.'' He grinned, his dark eyes lighting with amusement and love. "Neither of them is complaining about the time they have together. I spent two days with them and then decided I felt like a third on a honeymoon. Definitely not my style.'' He sipped his drink before changing the subject slightly. "The house is almost finished and their idea of incorporating Joy's work with Slater's seems to be working. Her knowledge of kidnappings and the kind of steps we all can take to avoid the situation is adding a dimension to Slater's elite security angle, and his reputation has opened some avenues for her.'' He smiled again. "It's a good, strong marriage with just enough pepper thrown in to keep the mixture from being bland. You did a good job with that match.'' He met her light blue eyes, lifting his glass in a silent toast.

"So when do you intend to give in and let me try my hand at your future?'' Her pale brows arched as she challenged him.

He tipped back his head, laughing, not taking her seriously in spite of her reputation as a consummate matchmaker. "I told you. I don't want or need a wife. I'm out of the country more often than I'm in. I don't have the energy when I am home to indulge in any real kind of relationship. Nor do I have the inclination.''

Her glance mocked him. "Are you certain that's all there is?''

Some of his humor died, caution raising its dependable head. "Meaning?"

"I can think of only one reason for a man with so much to give to close himself off from a permanent relationship."

A hit too close to home but he didn't show it. "Your imagination."

"Fact. I saw you with Joy as she sat so calmly in the hospital waiting room, so seemingly unmoved by the fact that your brother might very well have been dying. You were the only one who really reached out to her in spite of what all of you who didn't know her and her extraordinary emotional control must have been thinking. You have a tenderness for my sex that is rare. An intuition, although I doubt you would call it that. You talk like a cynic but I think that's an act."

He shrugged and set his glass aside. Slater had warned him this woman saw more than most. "So I love my brother and I had faith in his ability to know what he wanted in his life." He ignored the rest of her comments, deciding anything he said would leave him open for more of her probing.

"It could be that," she agreed, her writer's skill giving her the ability to read the smallest reaction. "But it also could be something else."

"I'm not going to stick my head in a noose of yours or anyone else's making."

"I haven't asked you to. In fact, all I had asked then, at the party for Slater and Joy, was for you to describe the woman you think you would like to spend your life with. Slater, or anyone for that matter, could have told you my influence extends only to the introduction.''

His eyes narrowed, finally taking her seriously. She looked like a wicked saint, sitting there with her blouse falling off her shoulders, her silver hair a veil of light about her calm face. Her pale eyes demanded his attention, her words teased his mind. For the last three months, he had thought nothing of her lightly thrown dare as they had stood in a room full of people celebrating his brother's hospital bedside marriage and his survival of a terrible accident. He had been too busy for one thing and frankly uninterested for the rest. And yet, what could be the harm? he wondered, recalling the way Slater had looked at his Joy, another of Pippa Luck's success stories. Did he really want to spend his life alone? He thought of his dream, his nightmare of wanting and never having. Slater's brush with death had touched him, changed him, creating questions where there had been certainty. What could it hurt? Besides, it might be interesting to see what Pippa thought, how she had spun Slater and Joy into her web.

''All right.'' He waited for the triumph and only received her total attention and silence waiting for him to fill it with an ideal. It took a moment for a mental picture of a woman he could love to form.

''I want a someone who is calm and peaceful. My professional life with Whitney-King is predicated on other people and their problems. Everything from local protest organizations to international squabbles end up being dumped in my lap with little or no warning. I don't want that in my home. I want someone who isn't given to making waves, setting me and others on their ears. Someone who doesn't take risks with her life for the sheer hell of it or because she has so many material things that she's jaded enough to need the adrenaline rush of pitting herself against the odds. Someone who doesn't lie in my arms so pliantly, so generously that I forget that beneath that soft skin beats the heart of a daredevil who delights in making my life one long stream of crisis. Someone who doesn't have red hair that reminds me of living flames and blue eyes that whisper of a peace that never happens when I'm near her. Someone who will at least listen when I beg her not to do something dangerous. Someone who won't end up dangling from a tree by a few slender ropes and then cut my heart out when I get her down to the ground."

He leaned back in his chair, remembering and wishing he could forget. His voice deepened, slowed so that for the first time since he'd begun his description, emotions leaked into the words, a waterfall of feelings pouring from the mind to the pool of silence waiting to receive them. "Someone who is easy to understand and easier to love."

One of Pippa's greatest gifts was her ability to listen when it really mattered. Because Slater had been her friend since she had married Josh, she knew of Stryker, his demanding job as head troubleshooter for the Whitney-King International Corporation, but until the accident that had almost claimed his triplet's life, she hadn't met the man himself. Then she had seen him accept Joy, seeing beyond her monumental control in impossible circumstances to the courage and heart of a woman fighting death in the only way she had. He had stood against his father and brother, reaching out to Joy for Slater's sake and for Joy's own. Pippa admired that kind of sight, of caring. From that moment on, Stryker had had her admiration and her interest. And yet the more she looked, the more she was aware of a deep well of loneliness and old pain. He smiled, touched his family, taking Joy as one of them. But through it all, he stood slightly aloof, not cold, just away, careful of getting too close, of being too vulnerable. Only a woman could have taught him that, a woman with red hair, blue eyes, and danger in her blood.

"What was her name?"

Because he was lost in his memories, because he hadn't realized he had given himself away, Stryker forgot the question wasn't a product of his own mind. "Tempest." The moment the silence embraced his curse, once his woman, he opened his eyes and glared at Pippa. "Damn you." The oath was without heat, making it all the more powerful.

"Probably." She stared at the glass in her hand. "Walking away never answers."

"In this case it does. I met the foe and learned her name."

She lifted her eyes to his. "No. You think you did but you haven't or you would be able to let her go. But you can't." She held up her hand when he would have interrupted. "She lives in your memory. A benchmark for other women. Not what you want but what you don't want."

"I know myself."

She smiled at that. "Do any of us really know ourselves? Did Slater, who didn't believe in tomorrow? Did Joy, who didn't believe that she could love without bringing death to the one she loved? Did I, who didn't believe that someone as conventional as Josh could love someone who always must be meddling in the lives of others, who spins tales of fantasy places and makes them real, who demands so much of those she loves because she will never be easy to love herself? We all proved we didn't know ourselves, our needs, and our hopes. We touched each other, learning, growing, changing, reaching out, and getting hurt but healing, too.''

Stryker rose and walked to the window, his back to her and the words that wouldn't change the past or write the future. ''It wasn't love.''

Her eyes were kind, understanding, and more knowing than he was. ''As you wish.'' She got to her feet and went to him. ''I know of a woman who fits your description. And you fit hers. Shall I invite her to even the numbers tonight?''

His dark brows arced, both at her release of a subject he would have bet his last suit she would pursue and at her offer. ''If you wish.'' Like Slater before him, he reminded himself that he didn't have to like whatever female was brought for his perusal. Meeting wasn't dating.

Pippa touched his arm, smiling faintly. ''Use the pool if you like. I have a call or two to make and a little to finish on the last chapter of the book. Will you mind?''

''No.'' He grinned at her, relaxing for the first time since she had dragged Tempest out of the dark room in his mind he kept walled off just for her. ''What time is dinner?''

''Seven and casual.'' She strolled to the door without looking back. If she had, she would have seen the rueful look in Stryker's eyes. It wouldn't have mattered to her plans but it would have made her laugh.

"Of course, I'll come to dinner, Pippa," Barbara Dane said, smiling faintly.

"It's more than dinner, actually."

Barbara sat down on the rattan chair beside the matching table. Sun streamed in the windows behind her, highlighting the Victorian decor of her bedroom. "How much more?"

"You remember when you and I discussed your love life."

"Or lack thereof," she murmured, beginning to get the drift of the conversation. "Are you telling me in typical Pippa style you've gone husband hunting?"

"Sort of."

"I thought you didn't agree with my ideas on the subject. In fact, as I recall, you were quite vehement on the matter. Something along the lines of my being shortsighted in my choices."

"I wasn't quite that blunt."

"Waffling, Pip?"

Pippa laughed. "No. I keep forgetting behind that ultra-ladylike manner lurks the mind of a shrewd woman."

"Investment counselors have to hear what's being said to them," she murmured mildly. "People have a tendency to get hostile when you mess around with their money." She paused and then added in an altered tone, "But to the main issue. Who is this man and why have you suddenly decided to stick to my ideas instead of those farfetched ones of yours?'' She frowned slightly, suddenly realizing that Pippa hadn't actually said she had stuck to anything. ''Or are you taking off on one of your famous Pippa-knows-best scenarios?''

''I wouldn't do that to you, or anyone come to that. I'm following your list to the letter. But before you meet Stryker, I'm making it clear I still don't agree with either of you on your requirements.''

Startled, Barbara stared at the landscape across the room, trying to decipher the nuances in Pippa's voice. ''This isn't a trick to get me to change my mind, is it?''

''No. But that doesn't mean I don't think you will anyway.''

''Is he a dog?''

Pippa grinned, wishing Stryker could hear that description. ''No. Handsome. Sexy with a voice to whisper lovely things in a feminine ear. A body to die for and enough sophistication to make any woman believe in aristocracy.''

''Sounds too good to be true.''

''You'll see tonight. If you're game.''

''I'll be there.''

''Josh will send a car.''

''That isn't necessary.''

''It might be if he decides to take you home and you decide to let him,'' she murmured before hanging up the phone. Pippa stared at the river view from her window, contemplating the unexpected complication in Stryker's life. Clearly, he didn't even understand his own feelings toward the unknown Tempest.

Of course, if half of what he had told her was true, the woman would be just the kind of female to drive a man like Stryker wild, make him doubt his own emotions and, perhaps, the attraction that existed as well. She smiled wickedly, wondering if Josh's network of associates included anyone or the daughter of anyone with the unlikely name of Tempest.

Stryker smiled at the woman seated beside him on the sofa. Dinner with Pippa and Josh had been relaxing and stimulating at the same time. Barbara Dane had been a pleasant surprise with her blond hair in a gleaming twist at her nape, her hazel eyes softly alight with humor, and a body that had enough curves to tempt a man into thinking of things not meant for the dinner table. She was smart, amusing, entertaining without being gushy, and soft spoken. She was clearly Pippa and Josh's friend, at home in this house by the river, comfortable with the wealth and power that Josh could command and the fame and outrageous behavior that surrounded Pippa like an invisible cloak.

Barbara flicked a discreet glance at her watch. "I really must be going," she said regretfully, finishing the last of her brandy.

Josh rose. "I'll call the car around."

Stryker got to his feet, looking down at her. He had enjoyed the evening but he wanted to see if more than just relaxation and mild pleasure was possible between them. "I'll take you home."

Barbara looked up at him, liking what she saw. The strength in his face appealed to her senses and his manners made a welcome change from the more brash of the male population that it always seemed her fate to meet. If there weren't any sparks, she considered that a point in his favor. She was tired of being burned by sexual attraction only to find once the fire was gone, nothing remained but a need to escape the cloying ties of a relationship with no future. "If you don't mind." She smiled.

He extended his hand, helping her to her feet. He waited for a reaction and found nothing in her touch that disturbed him. The faintest of frowns touched his brow. This was a good-looking woman, with all the things he had said he wanted, thought he needed. What was wrong with him, he wondered as they made their good-byes? He was still wondering after he dropped her off with a good-night kiss and an arrangement for lunch the following day.

He drove back to Josh's place, thinking of the women he had known since Tempest. Every one of them had a lot in common with Barbara Dane. Every one of them left him feeling as though something vital was missing and, until this moment, he hadn't known or, more accurately, hadn't wanted to know that something was wrong with the image of what he thought he needed. Damn Pippa for yanking Tempest out of his memories and holding her against his supposed ideal. He wouldn't allow his need of that red-haired daredevil to write the pages of his future. He would have no peace. Hell, he had none now, always wondering what she was doing and if she was surviving doing it. Living like that a man wouldn't be able to call his soul his own. Did he now? The answer wasn't reassuring. He couldn't have a home with Tempest, assuming he was crazy enough to try living with her. Anyone less capable of settling down he had yet to meet. He couldn't have children. Of course, he wasn't all that enamored of offspring at this point in his life anyway. He sighed, paced the guest room, and sighed again, thrusting his hand through his hair. He would go out with Barbara and do his best to stir some interest within himself. Now that he faced the problem, maybe, definitely he could put it behind him and go on with his life. He was certifiably nuts to continue allowing Tempest to dictate his companions and his tomorrow.

"I think you may have made another match," Josh observed as he watched his wife wander in from the bathroom, her robe draped about her slim, nude form. The displeasure in her expression was at odds with the sexy way she moved toward him and their bed.

"It looks that way."

He slipped the robe from her arms, his hands cupping her breasts as he drew her down to him. "Why do I think there is a large 'but' in there somewhere?" He arched her upper body toward his lips, blowing gently on the peaks budding so perfectly for his touch.

Pippa threaded her fingers through the hair on his chest and tugged gently. "Do you know anyone named Tempest?" she asked instead of answering directly.

At the unusual name, Josh halted in mid-caress, his eyes narrowing at Pippa's too casual tone. "Maybe."

She looked down at him, smiling through the fans of her lashes. "Don't stop."

"You expect me to concentrate on this when I know you and that diabolical brain of yours are up to something?" He kissed one taut nipple and fought the hot need that was snaking through him, fracturing his attention on her words. Pippa never asked idle questions nor did she ever walk a straight line when a crooked one was possible. He raised his head and stared into her eyes rather than at her bewitching body. A man had only so much willpower after all. "You've got to be kidding. What has Stryker been telling you about Tempest?"

"How do you know he told me anything?"

Josh rolled, bringing Pippa fully into bed so that she lay beside him and he was looking down at her. "Tempest is Arthur Whitney-King's daughter."

"Stryker's boss?"

"Got it in one."

Pippa looked into his eyes, past him, remembering the nuances in Stryker's voice. "So he's in love with the boss's daughter. With his pride that would be a problem."

Josh gave a short bark of laughter, stunned and amused at her farfetched conclusion. "Stryker in love with Tempest? This time I know you've lost your mind. That young woman was put on this planet to make every one of us believe fervently in planned parenthood. She's a bona fide eccentric. If there is anything off the wall or downright dangerous going on anywhere in the world, I promise you Tempest will be right in the middle of it. And the person dear old daddy most often calls to get his erring daughter out of whatever mess she's gotten into is Stryker. I doubt our friend finds Tempest anything but a pain in the rear.''

Pippa ignored the summation, fairly certain most of it was true. "How old is she?"

"Twenty-five now."

"And Stryker has worked for Whitney-King for twelve years."

"Ten of those years have apparently been spent chasing after Tempest."

"Why?"

"Tempest got into trouble at the private school she attended just after her fifteenth birthday. Stryker had been with the company close to two years by then and was already making a name for himself as a man who could get in and out of sticky problems so smoothly that there were no loose ends. Arthur sent him after Tempest. He saved her from expulsion, scotched the rumors of a midnight flit with a boy twice her age and with a filthy reputation, and even managed to turn the situation around so that it looked as though Tempest was trying to help another girl break up with this creep."

"It could have been true."

"By that time it didn't really matter. Tempest was trouble from the time she was born. Her family loves her but she has about as much in common with her silk and diamond relatives as a mule has with a horse. The resemblance is only superficial." He touched her cheek. "So you see, Stryker isn't likely to be in love with someone like Tempest no matter how attractive she might be."

"Is she?"

"So I've heard. I've never met her myself. The few business dealings I've had with Arthur have been mostly long distance and the couple of times I've been to his house I haven't seen Tempest, only the rest of the family. I liked them all." He brushed her lips, teasing her mouth. "Now, could we possibly get back to my favorite night game, seducing my wife?"

She wrapped her arms around his neck, filing away all the information for the moment. Some things worked better in daylight and some things, one man especially, worked better at night. "I don't know. It depends on how good your intentions are."

"My actions are better."

She laughed softly, the sound ending abruptly as he took her mouth in a way that stole everything from her and filled her yet again with his taste and the fire of his love.

Stryker studied Barbara as she perused the luncheon menu. She was no less superbly turned out than the night before. Every hair was in place, her suit the epitome of a successful woman. The restaurant Pippa had suggested was a perfect setting for her, discreet, elegant, and tasteful. He shifted restlessly in his chair, halting the betraying movement when she looked up, her brows lifted, a faint, questioning smile on her face.

"Is there something wrong?"

He shook his head. "Have you decided?"

"Fruit salad, black coffee."

Predictable, he thought, cursing silently at the condemnation that had its roots in the insidious doubts that Pippa had placed in his mind. Tempest would have tucked into the menu, ignoring the calorie count because she never would have considered the problem. She burned energy so fast that keeping weight on was difficult. Irritated with himself, determined to focus on Barbara instead of the red-haired, blue-eyed image dancing like a maniacal genie in his head, he revised his own menu choice along more conservative lines.

Barbara laid aside the bill of fare, her smile deepening. "I can't resist looking but I know better than to indulge."

"Healthy eating isn't something you have to apologize for."

"You're a nice man."

The words were soft, clearly sincere, but somehow lacking depth and that rush of air at the end of each sentence as though the speaker were in a hurry to get to the next phrase. Damn Tempest and his too clear memories. Damn Pippa for reminding him.

"You're a lovely woman." He smiled, leaning forward slightly, looking into her eyes, searching for a response that would trigger his own lagging interest. A moment later, the waitress arrived and he sat back as pleasantly partnered as the night before. He liked her poise, her conversation, the way her eyes stayed on him instead of searching the world around him, inhaling every movement of life, every high, every low.

The time they spent together was easy, undemanding, the ideal Stryker had been certain he wanted. He had told Pippa his needs and she had fulfilled them exactly. And just as exactly his reaction was as she predicted. He returned to the house on the river, mounting the stairs without meeting anyone. He walked into his room, slamming the door behind him. He wished he could blame his reaction on chemistry. He wished he could believe that another woman would make his blood run hot. He knew better. In the four years since Tempest had lain in his arms, giving herself with complete abandon, he had dated, even shared the night, with other women, not many but enough to know that somehow that red-haired dynamo had branded him hers forever. He didn't like the feeling and he sure as hell had fought it but truth was truth. So what did he do about it?

"Nothing," he muttered furiously, swinging away from the peaceful scene of the St. John's river flowing without end to the sea. "I've lasted this long. I can last until I either grow out of it or get too damn old to care about any woman."

———— TWO ————

"Kitty, where are the boxes of formula that were delivered yesterday?" Tempest demanded, striding into the small, primitive hut and searching the gloom for her friend. She found her in the corner, a tiny baby in her lap, a stethoscope tucked in her ears, and a beautiful smile on her face for the dark-skinned child who watched her so carefully.

"Should be in the shed behind the sleeping quarters," she said without looking up.

"I looked there. Nothing."

Kitty lifted her head then, frowning. "Are you sure?"

"Yes, I'm sure. I checked that whole shipment myself. Every item on your list arrived. I even watched José and Luis carry most of it into the shed." She yanked a sweat-dampened handkerchief from her back pocket and mopped her face. Her red hair was tied back in a pony tail, her shorts were khaki in a bush-cut style. Her blouse was button-up and cotton, a strip of wet between her shoulder blades and her breasts. Her face was bare of makeup and she had boots on that made her legs look more sleekly muscled than ever. She looked earthy, appealing, and, with the zest of living in her eyes, totally in command of her primitive environment.

"No one from the camp would steal from us."

"I don't think so either. Admittedly, I've only been here a week but these people love you and what you're trying to do for them and their children." She stomped over and flopped down on an upturned box. She made a funny face for the child, laughing with the same exuberance as the toddler at the effect.

Kitty watched them both, smiling, feeling the exhaustion that had been dragging at her flee before the rush of energy that followed and surrounded Tempest wherever she went. "We have to have that formula," she said rising, the child in her arms.

Tempest bounced to her feet and held out her hands. The baby launched himself at her, innocent trust in his outstretched body. She caught him close, swinging him in a wide arc that made him giggle.

"You're better than a dozen volunteers. You could make a sphinx laugh," Kitty murmured as she led the way out of the hut.

"Because I'm a clown."

"No, because you're you," Kitty stated flatly. She gestured to Luis. He came to her, his dark eyes as worried as her own. In Spanish, she asked him about the missing formula. His shrug was more eloquent than any words.

"Damn. What are we going to do? We have fourteen babies in the compound who need that."

"Wet nurses?" Tempest suggested.

"For one or two maybe."

"Goats," Tempest added.

"We ate them or have you forgotten? That shipment of supplies was almost a month late. With that uprising in the hills and the refugees fleeing their homes, there just isn't enough easily secured game to feed us," Kitty reminded her.

"I know it was either the herd or starvation. You made the only choice you could."

"And now we're paying for it. We have food for the adults but not for the babies," Kitty sighed tiredly.

"We could try going upriver into the village—it's closer than the city downriver—to buy some goats, maybe even some formula. If it was stolen by the black market people, then it might have found its way there," Tempest pointed out.

"No! Don't even think it. That place is crawling with military and the stories we've both heard don't indicate any finer feelings in the way they're treating women, American citizens or not." Kitty stabbed her fingers through her cropped blond hair. "I wish I had never let you talk me into allowing you to stay here. Your father will kill me if something happens to you."

Tempest grimaced but didn't dispute the truth. Her father would have everyone's head if one hair on her own was damaged regardless of whether it was her own fault or not. "You needed someone. I was here."

"You shouldn't have been. I couldn't believe it when you got off that airborne relic you chartered in here."

"I just wish I had known you were running so low on supplies. I would have brought stuff with me."

Kitty wrapped her thin fingers around the supple muscles of Tempest's arm. "Don't take any of the blame. You are the only reason we have any supplies at all. I don't know what you paid that mercenary for a turnaround trip, loaded to his eyebrows, but we have more stuff now than we've ever had. Food, blankets, medical supplies, dishes, clothes, and, once, formula."

"It was only money." She shrugged, uncomfortable with the topic. "Anyone would have done the same. Probably wouldn't have allowed that damn formula to wander off either. I know Stryker wouldn't have if he had been here," she added in disgust. "That still doesn't solve the problem."

"We'll do the best we can. Maybe there's some canned milk in the boxes of food. That's the only thing that wasn't item by item inventoried, wasn't it?"

The two women entered the shed and stared at the small mountain of cartons.

"I'll look. You go on with your health checks."

Kitty nodded. "I never said thank you."

"I wish you hadn't remembered now." Tempest stalked over to the closest box and ripped open the lid. "If Luis isn't busy, you can send him in to help. It will go faster with two."

Kitty watched her back for a moment, wishing,

not for the first time, that she truly understood her friend. Tempest seemed so straightforward but the moment anyone got close he or she discovered just how complex a personality she truly had. Take her relationship with Stryker. He was her nemesis or her rescuer depending on the situation. Tempest clearly admired him but equally, at times, she seemed to dislike him intensely. Kitty had once suspected that the two of them had been lovers. When asked, Tempest had never really answered her, but Kitty had never forgotten the swiftly disguised agony in Tempest's eyes. They had a history, closer than many marriages, but something was hurting Tempest, something connected with Stryker. And because Tempest was her friend, maybe her best friend in all the world, Kitty wished that she could sit Stryker down somewhere and demand an explanation. But she couldn't. One, because she'd never met the man. And more important, because Tempest would have her head for daring to interfere.

Kitty sighed, her gaze moving across the small haven she and the members of the relief force had carved out of the jungle around them. She couldn't help Tempest. In fact, smack dab in the middle of this mini-revolution, it was damn doubtful she could even help herself. A week ago, when the plane had been available to airlift them to safety, there hadn't seemed to be a need. There was always unrest in this part of the world. She had thought the small battles had been the same as had gone before. She had been wrong. The rumors were bad, very bad. And she was scared. They had no weapons, no protection, and, right now, no place to run. In short, they were sitting ducks.

"It's not working, is it?" Barbara lifted her head from Stryker's shoulder. The dance floor was crowded but the music was slow, making conversation possible.

Stryker looked down at her, knowing she felt the same lack of attraction as he. "I had hoped it would," he admitted finally, honestly. She was a fine woman and deserved better than forced, mild interest. "It's not you."

She smiled faintly at that, liking him more for the truth. She sighed, wishing things could have worked out. Much as she hated to think it, maybe Pippa was right, maybe she was looking in the wrong place for the wrong things. "Oddly enough, even though it may sound conceited, I didn't think it was. There is someone else in your mind and it isn't me."

The narrowing of his eyes was the only visible sign he gave that she had stumbled on the truth.

"Besides, Pippa warned me that no matter how sexy you are it wouldn't work for us." She glanced away for a moment, then back. "I hate it when she's right."

"I know the feeling."

"You, too?"

"Yeah." The music stopped. He cupped her elbow and escorted her back to their table. "I have enjoyed myself these last two days."

"So have I." She touched his hand. "I wish it could have worked for us. You really are a nice man."

He laughed softly at that. "Would you mind a piece of advice?"

She tipped her head, smiling a little at the question and the amused look in his eyes. "No."

"The next time you decide to compliment a man, skip the word *nice*. It tends to make us think of meek, mild, and boring. I can live with being sensitive, aware of a woman's needs. But I think most of my gender still have enough caveman in them to wish for something a little more stimulating than *nice* from the woman they're seeing."

"I'll have to remember that."

He glanced around, looking for a waiter.

Barbara stopped him with a touch. "No, don't. It's getting late and I really would like to go now."

"You're sure?"

"Yes. I have some thinking to do and, tonight, I find I want to do it." She rose gracefully. "You stay. I'll just call a cab."

"No. You aren't the only one who needs to think."

"He's back early." Pippa let the curtain drop as she moved from the window.

"Don't sound so pleased, wife. It might not mean anything more than Barbara needed an early night."

Pippa glared at her husband. "I can do without your brand of logic. He doesn't have that kind of expression on his face."

Josh wrapped his arms around his love and pulled her back against his chest. "Behave. You've unleashed your little scheme and, knowing you, it probably bore fruit, maybe even for both of them."

"That's only half the battle. There's still Tempest." She tipped her head to look up at him.

He dropped a kiss on her upturned lips. "Forget it. I have tried my damnedest to think of a way to bring them together and there isn't one. Besides, knowing of Tempest, chances are she'll manage that feat on her own."

"When she's in another mess. That's just going to make it worse." She turned in his arms, jumping slightly when the phone rang. Josh reached past her to answer. She felt the tension in his body and the sudden anxiety flowing into his expression. Her fingers tightened on his arms.

"Hold on, Arthur." He cupped his hand over the receiver. "Get Stryker, honey. Fast. It's his boss."

Pippa didn't waste time asking questions. She ran out of the study and up the stairs. One knock and she was in his room without waiting for an answer.

Stryker came out of the bathroom, his shirt open to the waist, his shoes off. "Pippa?" he said in surprise. "What's wrong?"

"Your boss is on the line. Something serious."

Stryker strode to the phone and punched the lit button. "What is it, Art?"

"It's Tempest." His usually self-assured voice broke, then steadied with a deep sigh. "She's missing. This isn't something small, Stryker. She's in Central America, near the border of Nicaragua."

"Hell."

"Exactly. You know what kind of unrest is down there. She's right in the middle of it."

"How? The last I heard she was in Switzerland."

"She has a friend who's a doctor with one of the

private relief organizations. She was on her way home from Rio and decided to stop in to say hello. As far as I've been able to find out, she chartered a plane into the compound and then sent it back for supplies. She didn't come out, and four hours ago, an embassy official called to tell me word had come downriver that the camp had been overrun by the rebels, the locals scattered, and one of the two doctors killed. There was no sign of Tempest." He paused, then forced out the last words. "We don't know if she was taken or escaped. We don't care what it takes, how long, how much but find her for us, Stryker. Name what you need and we'll move heaven and hell to get it for you."

It was a command and a desperate plea.

"A way into the area and weapons."

"Taken care of. The embassy will give you every cooperation. The company jet is already on the way to you and I'm faxing you a complete report of everything I was told, directions to the camp, and as many names as might be helpful."

Stryker frowned at the transport delay that couldn't be helped. He didn't dare risk chartering unknown equipment and personnel. "All right. Let me know if there's any more news."

"Stryker . . ." The man hesitated uncharacteristically. "No matter what happens, I won't forget you tried."

Stryker didn't answer. Both knew there were no promises for this mess, only desperate hope and desperate measures. He turned to head for the closet to begin packing. Josh stood in the doorway.

"I heard. You don't have to wait for King's plane.

Use mine. Greg, my pilot, flew in 'Nam. He's tough and he won't crack if it gets messy down there.''

"You're sure?"

"Sure enough. The plane's already being pre-flighted. Greg is either at the field or so close it doesn't matter. Pippa's putting some food together for you, and Rich is setting up a med pack and some concealed armament in the plane itself. He'll be waiting at the field to show you where. Christiana is tending to the hiking gear and supplies. All you need to do is throw your clothes in the case and be at the front door in five minutes. The car's waiting. We'll take care of your rental.''

Stryker accepted his help with a curt nod as he tossed shirts and slacks at the bag lying open on his bed. Josh collected his toilet articles.

"Rich offered to go with you. And so will I.''

Stryker shook his head. "Thanks for the offer but no. The less fuss the better. A group is too damn easy to spot. One in, two out.''

"If half of what I've heard is true, Tempest is tough. And she's got courage.''

Stryker snatched the zipper of the bag closed and straightened, looking Josh in the eye. "Yeah. Too damn much guts. She'd charge hell with a teaspoon of water and a glint in her eye. She's a five-foot-two stick of uncontrollable human dynamite. If the doctor who was killed in that godforsaken corner of the world was her friend and Tempest is still out there running loose, she'll be tracking her friend's killers. She won't give up and she won't walk away to save her own neck,'' he prophesied hoarsely. "And if they do have her, she won't bend. She'll let them break her, any way they have to but she won't bend." His face twisted in the agony of knowing just what could be happening to her.

Josh caught his shoulder, his hand strong and demanding. "I've married a strong woman. I understand what you're saying. But know this. The very strength you fear is the only damn defense she's got. Her only chance until you can get to her."

"I'll get her out or die trying." He hefted his suitcase and stalked to the door.

Pippa was waiting in the foyer. "The food's in the car, some for now and later." She reached up to kiss his cheek, her pale eyes compassionate. "Make sure you eat."

"I will."

Tempest rolled over groggily, spitting the dirt and leaves out of her mouth as she lifted her throbbing head gingerly from the ground. Every bone in her body ached. Her mouth was drier than the Sahara and her clothes were sticking to her with a combination of blood and sweat. The smell of fire and jungle mixed in a sickening concoction, making her dizzy. She bit her lips against moans of pain as she carefully checked her extremities for injury. Sweat was beading on her forehead by the time she had finished but at least the news was good. She was reasonably intact. Now what was she doing, lying on her back in the middle of the day in the density of the underbrush? She eased into a sitting position by stages, her lashes shut against the vertigo that made her wish she had never attempted to change position. Only an urgency she didn't understand drove her on. Finally, swaying slightly, her hands braced on the ground on either side of her hips, she gained some control over herself. Sounds started to impinge on her mind, screams, shouts, gunfire, explosions. Hell had broken loose in the green silence. Frowning, Tempest risked lifting a hand to brush aside the limbs shielding her just enough to allow her to see the outside world.

Orange flames clawed at the trees, shriveling the leaves, the flowers, anything they touched. She inhaled sharply, suddenly remembering enough of the last few minutes to understand what was happening. The camp had been attacked, first by grenades or something like them, then men, yelling, shooting at anything that moved. She had been in the shed. Hearing the commotion, she had run out. Suddenly the world had been all earsplitting noise and light. Flying through space ending in a sickening slam into the earth. Then no more. Until now.

The shed was gone. The camp burning and an absence of war were invading the clearing as the rebels gathered, laughing, calling to each other in a celebration of their victory over their foe. Tempest stared at them, realizing that she was very probably the only one spared. She wondered vaguely why God had made such a poor choice. Better Kitty or the other doctor. Or one of the children who had yet to taste the richness of life. Tears rolled down her dirty face but she didn't notice. She saw only the destruction of good by the forces of man's cruelty and heard only the laughter of the victor over his vanquished. She watched as the man in command sent groups out in twos to search the area for survivors. Crouching in the dense brush, she snuggled into the natural rock and root hollow that was her only shelter. She didn't think they would come to this place, for it was visibly too rough an area for anyone to pass on foot. She wondered vaguely how she would get out if or when she ever got the chance. Waiting, tense, silent, often almost afraid to breathe, she strained her ears for the betraying sounds of the band leaving. Instead, she heard the group dig in, build a fire, and make preparations to stay.

Easing out of her hole, Tempest stared through the limbs, wishing the coffee brewing on the open fire didn't smell so good. She was hot, tired, in pain, and damn hungry. It was only because she had just jammed two cans of insect repellent in her pockets before she had left the shed at the beginning of the attack that she wasn't being eaten alive by bugs. Small mercies but in this country, small was sometimes the most you could hope for. She crouched lower as one of the perimeter guards strolled past her hiding place. The small gully had afforded her protection but it had also become a prison. She couldn't slip away because even if she could climb out she'd have to make enough noise to attract attention. So she waited.

The muted roll of thunder drew her attention to the sky. Rain. She smiled. At least this time she was in a mess, the gods had decided to be kind. Another of her problems, water, was solved for the moment. Now, if she could just find something to catch the moisture in. She glanced around, using her hands more than her eyes in the gathering gloom of the day slipping into night. Her fingers touched something hard, smooth, curved. She scraped the debris from around it, her smile deepening as she recognized the shape. A child's ball. The one that had gotten lost when she had tried to teach the older children a game. She felt for the pocket knife that Stryker had given her when she turned seventeen, the year she had gotten tangled in the parachute ropes and almost killed herself before she could untangle the mess to open her reserve chute. Stryker had made her promise that she could leave anything behind, her bra, her money, her passport, her shoes, but keep the knife close. And she had. It was the last thing to leave her possession at night and the first to return in the morning. It had gone on dates and adventures, helping her almost as much as Stryker had.

Touching it brought him close. Her eyes darkened, secrets that she never shared glowing in the blue depths. So like the rest of her family, loving her in spite of herself, caring for her, deploring her lifestyle, her need to grasp everything life had to offer. She shook her head, her lips taking on a sad droop that no one had ever been privileged to see. Tempest never cried. She raced the wind, charged the storm, and held time in her hands. But she never cried, never looked back, and never tried to demand anything of anyone. Man had been created free, untamed, gloriously unique in all the animal kingdom. He had no boundaries beyond those he fashioned for himself. He had no flaws beyond those he gave to others and he had no virtues except those seen by others of his kind. She lived this belief, held it close, and gave it to herself. Her life wasn't to be measured in a few short years of existence on this planet, but rather in what she could learn of herself and others. So she searched, knowing the questions but not the answers, knowing also that it was the journey, not the destination, that wore importance like a king's crown of office. She stroked the knife, wishing she could have reached out to Stryker, been brave enough to let him into her thoughts. But she hadn't. That morning when she had crashed the hang glider she had been seized by the need to run as fast and as far as she could, to slip the bounds of earth and soar across the sky in true free flight. Even then, she had prayed that he would understand. Even then, she had known as the sky rained its tears upon her that he would not. His way and hers only met when destiny decreed another rescue.

Shaking off her futile thoughts, she set about carving a hole in the ball as the first drops of rain hit. A leaf of a banana plant became a wide-mouth funnel. Tempest lifted her face to the sky, her mouth open to catch the moisture even as her makeshift canteen started to fill with life-giving water. If his name was on her lips, only the jungle and the crying sky heard it.

Hours dipped by as steadily as the unceasing rain, shielding her from discovery but pulling precious body heat out of her. She did her best to fashion a tiny tent of leaves, affording her shivering body some protection, but she knew that it wasn't enough. By morning, as the sky cleared and the camp roused, her skin was clammy, her face flushed. She watched the men gather everything they could carry and prepare to leave. It was almost twenty-four hours since the attack. She had passed being hungry hours ago and every bone or muscle in her body was protesting the abuse it had suffered since yesterday. But she was alive and she intended to stay that way. With her eyes narrowed against the sun that was brighter than she remembered, she waited, unprepared to believe that just because she couldn't see anyone about didn't mean that the rebels had truly left the area. Finally, when it was well past noon, she began to search for a way out of her hiding place. An hour, several ripped nails, and a few hundred inventive curses later, she wiggled on her belly up and over the small rim that had been only eyebrow high but might as well have been as tall as Everest. She lay panting in the dirt, feeling the congestion gathering in her chest.

"I'm not having a cold now," she wheezed, dragging herself to her feet. "I don't have time. Or the energy." She stumbled toward the camp, even in her rapidly weakening state taking care to stay undercover. Now, if those rebels had just left something in the way of supplies and gear, she had a chance of getting out of this mess. There was a city downriver, by water a little more than a day's journey. On foot, it was probably three or four times that. She sighed deeply, then stifled a cough as she started a systematic search of the camp. Slowly, a pile of usable items grew. She stopped frequently as the sun got hotter and she got weaker. She needed food. But not here or now. First the supplies, then another hiding place, and then she would eat and rest.

THREE

Stryker walked into the main office of the embassy, ignoring the elegant decor that told of money well spent over many generations of a class that appreciated fine things. He was dressed in black, his face hard with purpose, his movements those of a male on the prowl and not afraid of anything he would find in the dark.

A swarthy, slim man rose from his chair behind the desk and extended his hand. "I am Ramón Valdez. It was I who called Arturo King."

Stryker took his hand, disguising his irritation with the necessity for wasting time on something so unimportant as introductions. "Any more information?" he asked briefly.

Sympathy lay in Ramón's dark eyes. He inclined his head. "A few facts only."

"The doctor who was killed was one of them I hope?"

He nodded again. "A man."

Stryker released his breath in a long sigh. Maybe, just maybe Tempest was trying to find a way out and not hunting those who had ambushed her friend. "And the other?"

"She was brought downriver late last night. She is here, resting."

"I'd like to see her."

"Of course. But she can tell you nothing about Señorita King. She knows only that her friend was in the supply shed and that it was blown up."

"Have you been able to get men into the area yet?"

"No. The doctor was taken out of the compound by a man named Luis. He got her to the river and on a boat down to us."

"Where is this Luis?"

Ramón spread his hands. "This I do not know. The doctor told us that he went back to help his people. We do not know if he still lives."

"And the man who handled the boat?"

"Waits here until the rebels return to the hills. I will take you to the good doctor now, but I must warn you that it is dangerous what you intend to do. We cannot send men with you nor after you should you be captured. The rebels are not kind to those of your country."

"All the more reason I must get to Miss King." He followed Ramón from the room and up the stairs to the bedroom wing. After knocking, Ramón opened the door, allowing Stryker to go in but staying in the hall himself.

Kitty lay propped up in bed, a livid bruise obscuring the right side of her face. Numerous cuts and scratches decorated the rest of her visible skin. "I hope to God you're Stryker," she said, tears pooling in her eyes.

Stryker came to the bed, taking the hand she held out to him. "I am."

"Then you will be able to get Tempest out of there."

"I'm going to do my best." He sat down gently on the bed, not sure how badly she was injured. "You think she's still alive." Her fingers squeezed his to the point of pain. He didn't notice.

"I won't let myself believe anything else. I know I didn't see her in the open and I know that she was in the shed looking for some baby formula that had disappeared. Luis was with her. He got out. She must have too. Besides, you know Tempest. She always gets out of trouble, no matter how bad," she whispered, her voice breaking as she turned her face into the pillow and started to cry. "I should have sent her out of there. We knew there was fighting. But the children needed so much. She got us supplies, I don't know how, and pitched in as though she had slugged it out in the wilderness all of her life. She laughed at the bugs, the food shortage, and the deprivations. She made the children smile. Made us smile." She raised her head, her eyes begging for his understanding, his forgiveness. "You know her. You know how she would dare God to tell her no. She can't be dead. So much life can't be gone."

Stryker gathered her in his arms, giving her what Tempest would have given had she been there. Comfort and a never-say-die belief. "If there is a way to survive, Tempest will find it. She'll get that damn-I-can-do-anything grin on her face and take on the jungle without a thought. She's strong and she's stubborn. She knows how to handle herself in primitive conditions and how to eat off the land. That's more than a lot of men.''

Kitty raised her head from his shoulder. ''You do know her. You hurt her so much. I was prepared to hate you. But you know her. How could you leave her?'' If she had been herself, she never would have pried. This man was strong, the kind of male that a woman who was a stranger to him did not question. He gave his answers only to those who were buried in his soul.

Stryker laid her back against the pillows. ''This isn't the time.''

''When you find her, make the time.'' For Tempest, for the debt she owed, she looked him in the eye, demanding what wasn't her right.

He rose, looking down at her. He didn't want to think that he had really hurt Tempest. Nothing in the last four years said that he had. Their relationship, in spite of that one small week, had gone as before. Tempest had been no different, no less dangerous, no more settled. If she cried, he had never seen it or heard of it. If she wished things had been different, she had never shown him that either. Her exploits had continued and he had continued to pull her out when she miscalculated. End of story. Beginning of heartache, his. ''That's between Tempest and me,'' he said finally.

She shook her head. ''Maybe you don't know her after all.''

"Do any of us?"

"No. But you have the best chance because I believe she wants you to understand her."

He raked his fingers through his hair as he headed
for the door. "Hell, she doesn't understand herself.
What chance do I have?"

"Maybe the only chance for either one of you, or
haven't you ever thought of that?"

Turning, Stryker stared at her, wishing he hadn't
thought of it or heard her bring to mind what he had
only just stumbled onto. "My priority is getting her
out. The rest isn't important now."

Kitty let the exhaustion sweep over her. She
doubted she would have had the strength to fight him
even when she was at full power. "You're right."

Stryker stared at her for one moment, then left the
room, closing the door gently behind him. In less
than an hour he faced the man who had brought the
doctor downriver, and with the persuasion of two
fifty-dollar bills, he bargained for a ride upstream to
a place less than a mile from where he had been
hailed by the missing Luis. The journey would be
longer because of the current and the lack of a motor
on the boat and also because, for safety's sake, they
would travel only at night. From the drop-off point
he would be on his own to find Tempest in her jungle
haystack.

"Señor, down!" the boatman hissed urgently.

Stryker dropped to the bottom of the small canoe,
yanking the smelly tarp over his head and body.
They were close to shore, close enough for anyone
to spot the occupants of the only craft on the river

that wound like a lazy serpent through the area.
Night wrapped kind shadows about them. So far, in
their journey, they had passed only two small groups
of rebels and been ignored by both. The boatman
had protested loudly and at length about the foolish
American set on getting him killed trying to get one
stupid woman out of a place where she should not
have been. Since he couldn't dispute the opinion,
Stryker hadn't even tried to reason. He had simply
extracted four more fifties and slapped them in the
man's dirty palm. The complaints had ceased and the
boat had moved on again. All total, it had been almost four full days since the attack. Stryker tried to
think not of the time, only the destination. Like
Kitty, he couldn't accept that the star that was Tempest had been burned out.

"How much farther?" he demanded from his hiding place.

"The next curve," the man returned roughly.

"That is the agreed-on drop?" Stryker lifted his
head enough to glare at his guide. The flicker in the
man's eyes told the truth even if his mouth did not.

"Sí." He licked his lips.

"Like hell. We made a bargain."

"I will go no farther. I am a family man."

"Bull." Stryker reached for his automatic.

The man paled. "Por favor, señor, it is true. I am
close to the drop, as you call it. Es verdad. Only
two miles. It is better for us both."

Stryker studied him closely. After a tense moment,
he decided the man was telling the truth. "All
right."

The guide's face conveyed his relief. "Cover now.

We must take care. The night is silent so that she may hear those who hide in her shadows.''

Stryker grimaced at the primitive poetry that was all too accurate. He couldn't help counting the hours since the camp had been attacked. The urge to rush in was almost overwhelming. But he knew the necessity of caution and stealth. Tempest's life depended on his ability to curb his rage and use his brain to its fullest. Stiffening as he felt the boat nudge the shore, he waited for the all clear. It came in a hiss that had no decipherable word. He rose, a shadow to blend with the other shadows shielding them from unfriendly eyes. He pressed an extra fifty into the boatman's hand as he passed.

"Vaya con Dios," the man whispered as he pushed away from shore without a ripple in the black river.

Stryker pulled on the infrared glasses that magnified the smallest light to turn night into day. He slipped into the jungle, using the compass and his own sense of direction to guide him. The sounds of prowling, nocturnal animals followed his progress, but other than to register their noise, Stryker ignored them. Sweat dripped down his back and face. He didn't stop. So little time.

He found the camp just before dawn. He read the signs of the battle, the small encampment later, and finally, because he had quartered the area so carefully, he found traces of Tempest. Her footprint beside the remnants of a tent, evidence that someone had carefully searched and stripped the camp of the smallest useful items that could be carried easily in a pack. He found where a torn tent had provided squares of canvas and scuff marks beside it where someone might have sat to stitch together a makeshift pack. His lips tilted in a grin that could have been a match for hers did he but know it.

"Now where the hell did you go, Tempest? You must have known about the city below you. And you can read signs fairly well, so you had to know the rebels seem to be moving away from the river." He glanced toward a path leading back toward the river, different from the one he had used coming into camp. "I hope I'm right." He shifted his shoulders, settling his own pack in a more comfortable position, then headed for the trail. He had gone only thirty feet when he saw the newly carved marks on a tree just off to the right.

STRIKE DN RIV 2 3 P

He stared at the shorthand that was uniquely Tempest's. His name. Downriver. Second day after the attack. Three P.M. He glanced at his watch. It was dawn of the fourth day. She had a hell of a start but he would find her. Relieved, he pushed on, moving as rapidly as was safe, always watching the trees for messages of her passage. He found the second and her camp of the first night. He stared at the small hollow that had held her fire, disturbed by how little distance she had come. Tempest should have moved faster. Unless she was hurt. He scoured the camp, finding no traces that indicated someone caring for any kind of injury. Extracting some dried food from his pack, he continued, his eyes narrowed, his mind sorting through possibilities and not liking anything he could find. Suddenly he stopped, staring at the long skid on the debris-strewn trail. No roots or boulders lay in the way. Nothing to account for the fact she had fallen. Uneasy, no longer feeling as relieved as before, he slugged down three swallows of water, tied a bandanna around his forehead to keep the sweat out of his eyes, and picked up his pace. Her next sign was not as carefully chosen as the other, nor was the carving as strong and sure. He traced the crooked letters, his face set in grim lines. He had picked up almost twelve hours on her in the six he had been traveling. She was barely moving. She was sick, probably feverish and weak. He swore softly, angrily, fearfully, aware of the strength ebbing from his own body at the killing pace he was forcing out of it. He would have to stop soon or risk going down himself.

"One more hour," he promised. "Stop Tempest. Wherever you are, wait for me."

Tempest stumbled, slamming to her knees in a fall that seemed to knock the breath right out of her. Thinking was difficult and moving almost impossible, but she forced both out of herself. She had to remember to leave Stryker a sign of her direction. She had to keep the river to her right and she had to pay attention to her surroundings. She was free and she would stay that way until either she reached the town on her own or Stryker found her.

"Stryker." As she heaved herself erect, his name was her prod. He was the one who had yelled the loudest about her chance taking, but he was also the one who had taken her to his brother Slater and demanded a course in survival skills that was just short of sadistic. She had cursed him then and since, but she blessed him now. "You'd better be looking for me," she panted, swaying drunkenly forward. "Yell. Scream. Don't care. Just find me." Even as the last words whispered off her lips, she fell forward, her body no longer strong enough to obey her will. With her last ounce of strength she rolled off the path into and under the foliage beside it, doing her best to hide herself. Her lashes closed, the only spots of color in her pale face. Unconscious, she didn't feel the night begin to wrap around her like a warm cloak.

FOUR

Stryker shrugged out of his pack and dropped Indian style down on the ground, drawing in great drafts of air. For the last hour he had been all but trotting, every step sending a greater message of urgency than the one before. Tempest was close. He could feel it. But he was just worn out. He had to rest. Glancing at his watch, he allowed himself an hour. He'd eat, relax as best he could, take a nap, then he'd push on. As near as he could figure, she wasn't more than two hours in front of him at his pace. His plan made, he carried it out to the last letter. When he awoke forty-five minutes later, he was still tired but not drained. He slaked his thirst, yanked on his pack, pulled on his infrared glasses, and got to his feet. Two more hours. Less if she made camp early.

He almost missed it. Hardly daring to breathe, he stared at the faint imprints of knees, hands, then a funny sideways roll. He bent down, carefully pushing aside the leaves of the plants shielding her. Tempest lay on her side, her body completely relaxed, her breath anything but. Stryker touched her face, feeling the fever raging in her system. He cursed roughly but he lifted her into his arms with the tenderness of a mother with her child. He held her close to his warmth and called her name.

Tempest heard his voice slipping through the fire that seemed to encase her in some terrible prison where there was no parole. She moaned, coughing. "Stryker?"

He winced at the broken sound, the congestion he could hear in her chest. They were too damn far away from help. He had medicine but he was working in the dark. Fear walked hand in hand with frustration and anger but only concern and gentleness laced his voice as he stroked the matted hair back from her face. "Open your eyes, sweetheart."

"Hurts."

His fingers traced her features, the pale lips, the bruised cheek and jaw. "I know, baby. But I need to see your pupils. You've got a bump on your head." He stroked the tangled red hair back from the area, gently probing without causing pain.

Her lashes flickered, then lifted. She tried to smile but her lips wouldn't listen to her heart. "Knew you'd find . . ." She coughed again, this time hard enough to hurt. ". . . me," she finished weakly when she could breathe again.

"You left a good trail." He kept her talking as he shone a tiny light in each of her eyes. "I told you Slater's course would come in handy one day."

She laughed softly, the amusement ending in another more violent spate of coughing. "Hate told-you-sos."

He tucked the light in one of the zippered pouches on his leg. "Shut up," he ordered, cradling her closer as she started to shiver. "Save your strength."

"Okay," she whispered docilely, suddenly feeling the world begin to slip away again. "Always take care of me." The second she finished the last word she slept.

Stryker stared at her washed out face, knowing that he had never seen her look so damn good. He had thought he had lost her forever. Being careful not to jar her, he rose with her in his arms. He continued down the trail, searching in the darkness for a place to lay her head so that he could care for her. They needed shelter and rest.

"Hot! So hot!" Tempest whimpered, trying to squirm away from the fire that singed her body. Chains held her down. She cried out. A voice, strong, deep, familiar answered.

"Lie still, baby. Lie still." Stryker held her down, wrapping the covers over the part of her he wasn't sponging down with boiled water from the river. She was naked under the blankets, scratched, bruised, burning up with a fever that the antibiotic he had injected had yet to touch. But she had no concussion that he could detect.

"Stryker?" Tempest forced open her eyes, at first seeing nothing but darkness.

"Here, baby. Right here." He leaned closer, brushing her lips with his.

"Dreaming?"

"No." He wrung out the cloth from the small bowl he had created out of a makeshift ball canteen. He drew it gently over her bruised face and down her throat. Her sigh of pleasure was one of the sweetest sounds he had heard in a long time. "You've got a fever, sweetheart. I've pumped you full of antibiotics but they won't be counting in until tomorrow." He spoke slowly, clearly so that the words would penetrate. Dropping the cloth in the bowl, he slipped his arm under her shoulders and raised her carefully so that she was braced against his chest. Beside him was a cup with aspirin dissolved in liquid. He lifted it to her lips. "Drink this."

Tempest tried to free her hands from the blankets but she just wasn't strong enough, so she let him feed her. The water tasted strange but cool. She sipped thirstily, finishing it all.

"Good girl." Liking the feel of her against him, needing the reassurance of holding her, he tucked the blankets more firmly around her and went back to his sponging. First her face and throat and then each arm, her side, a breast, the soft silk of her stomach, then begin again. He lost count of the times he passed the cloth over her heated flesh. The moments were measured in her sighs of relief and the touch of her skin to his. He knew the instant she fell asleep in his arms. He knew also that he and the medicine had yet to gain enough strength to fight the fever that had a stranglehold on her body. His face grew grimmer as the night wandered toward dawn. And still the fever climbed. Her sleep faded into delirium.

*   *   *

"No Stryker. Not on purpose. Promise."

Stryker grabbed Tempest's hands as she tried to throw off the blankets. She was shivering, crying tears he had never seen her shed, and every nightmare that her fever-racked body had relived had begun and ended with his name. He lifted her into his arms, feeling the same sigh drift past her lips that had come every time he held her. She turned her face into his neck, nestling against him as though she had come home. Her breath was hot on his flesh but he held her tightly anyway. Suddenly she started to quiver, her voice breaking with words that made little sense. She was cradled against him now as the crisis surged over her. Sweat stood out on her flesh, her moans, her torment almost more than he could bear, but bear it he did, for her sake. He didn't know, wouldn't have cared if he had known, that he crooned gently, soft and low to her, his voice wrapping her in sound as surely as his arms held her safe.

The fever broke. A silence as complete as the darkness in the center of a moonless midnight cloaked him as he rocked her tenderly. Her breathing was labored but seeming to ease a little. Her lashes flickered, then slowly lifted. He traced her lips delicately, smiling as she focused so carefully on his face.

"Welcome back," he whispered.

"Thirsty."

"Good." He reached for the cup he kept filled beside him, this time with more aspirin. Raising it to her lips, he let her sip.

"Tastes funny." She lay back against him, the small effort draining what little strength she had.

"Aspirin."

She closed her eyes, his scent as familiar as his arms. She felt safe as she always did when he was near. Then she remembered the camp. Her eyes opened, revealing panic that she wouldn't have shown if she had been herself. "We can't stay. Rebels."

"I know." Stryker tucked the blankets more securely around her. "They are heading away from us at the moment."

"Don't trust them." She fumbled for his hand through the folds of the blanket.

Her grip was pitifully weak but nothing in Stryker's expression betrayed his worry. He touched her lips, silencing her before she could protest any more. "We're fine here for now. I promise. Stop wasting your energy. Sleep."

"You?"

"Yes, I'll sleep too."

She searched his eyes, her thoughts chaotic. Something wasn't right but she couldn't figure out what. "Promise?"

Covering her eyes with a gentle hand, he said, "Hush, woman. Sleep now. So I can."

A smile trembled at the edge of her mouth. "Okay."

He watched her, sighing as he felt her body relax in his arms. It would be dawn in another hour. He was tired, not exhausted yet but getting close. It had been four days since he had done more than catnap. There was no telling how much longer it would be before he could get her to safety. And until he did, he couldn't afford to let down his guard. Like her, he had no great faith in the rebels staying out of reach. Studying her sleeping face, he listened to her breathing. She was due for another shot of antibiotics in two hours. With any luck and a lot of praying, she might be able to handle being moved sometime tomorrow. He'd have to carry her and that would slow them down, increase the risk of them being spotted, but he had no choice. Travel by night was his best chance and he intended to use it. Settling her more comfortably against him, he leaned back against the rock that seemed to have become his chair. His gun lay at his side, ready for use. Closing his eyes, he relaxed his body but left his senses on alert for intruders.

Tempest stretched carefully, feeling weak but definitely better than she had the day before. She was alone in the tiny clearing, encircled by the jungle. A canteen lay close. It took enormous effort to slip her arm out of the blanket and pull the canvas-covered container close. The lid was loosened but not loose enough to allow leakage. She smiled faintly. Stryker thought of everything. Sipping carefully, even though the canteen had little more than a few sips in it, she let the liquid chase the unbelievable dryness from her parched mouth.

"You're looking better," Stryker said as he walked silently into the campsite. He dropped a three-fish string on a banana leaf and then came down on his knees beside her. "Feel like a little breakfast?" He took the canteen from her and recapped it.

"Those?"

"You like fish." He turned to reach for the covered pot that was cooling to one side of the small fire he had made before leaving for the river.

Tempest watched the smooth play of the muscles of his back as he filled the canteen with boiled water and placed it next to her. "I would have been happy with anything."

He grinned as he turned back to her. "That bad?"

A cough stole her answer. He was frowning when she finally caught her breath enough to look at him again. "Stop worrying. I feel a lot better than I did yesterday." She started to lift her hand. He captured it before she could complete the effort. "Weak but better. I'll be all right after I eat."

Stryker wanted to argue with her. Her independence had always been a bone of contention between them. He knew what she was doing now. She understood the danger and was hell-bent to prove she could be on her feet and moving before the day was out.

"Let's wait and see," he murmured after a moment.

Startled, for she had expected a flat denial, Tempest stared at him suspiciously.

He laughed softly at the look in her eyes. "Blue lasers."

"What?"

"Your eyes remind me of blue lasers when you start trying to figure out what's on my mind." He bent and kissed her gently, laughing again at the soft gasp of surprise she couldn't control.

"What was that for?"

"Pleasure."

He rose and moved to his catch, aware that Tempest was watching him closely. With his back to her, he smiled to himself. He had made mistakes without number in dealing with her on a personal level. He didn't understand her, and for the first time in his life, he knew that he had to if he was ever to reach her. Last night had taught him what all the years, all the curses, and all the wanting had not. Somehow, this scrap of femininity was made to share his life. He didn't know how. He sure didn't know when or where. He wasn't even positive he could convince her to see things his way but he was going to find the keys to her needs that had eluded him all these years. He was tired of living on the edge of wanting to wring her neck for the chances she took. He was past being able to chase her around the world without wishing he had the right to demand that she come home to him. He wanted her. That one fact had made his dreams more nightmares. That one fact had made other women impossible substitutes. That one fact had made walking away from her impossible. And that one fact had driven him past the point of biding his time, waiting for her to tame the wildness in herself. It was time he gentled her, reached past the barriers he sensed but didn't understand to help her come into her own. So there would be no more confrontations. He would try reason and diversionary tactics. He would use the finesse that had gained him the respect of his peers and success in his professional life. And he would win. Tempest would see that life with him was what she wanted. The storms that had haunted her youth would die. Her passion would satisfy her and him. He would give her the world and she would find it good.

"More?"

Tempest lay back against the air pillow, her empty plate on her blanket-covered stomach. "No. I'm stuffed."

Stryker took the dish and stacked it with his own. "It's time for more aspirin." He uncapped the bottle and tipped two into his palm.

"I'll take them the regular way." She held out her hand.

He gave her the pills, watching as she popped them in her mouth before washing both down with water. She still looked ill, but there was more life in her eyes and her voice was stronger. The cough and the congestion were still with her but the fever hadn't returned with any force. She was slightly warm but apparently on the mend. But she was still very weak. Her hands shook with every effort.

Tempest shifted restlessly under his probing stare. She knew she hadn't hidden from him the lack of strength that still made her feel like sleeping the day away. "How are we going to travel? Day or night?"

"Night." He waited, studying her, trying to get into her mind.

"Then I'd better get some sleep." She slid down in the bed, glad for the excuse that wouldn't cost her any more face.

"We aren't going tonight."

Her eyes, on the point of closing, popped open. Her temper had never been her most dependable trait.

Illness hadn't improved the iffy situation in the slightest. "Why?"

Stryker read her anticipated reaction, feeling as though he was beginning to learn her. His excuse was ready, simple, and irrefutable. "I damn near killed myself catching up to you."

She frowned at that, skeptical of the answer but unable to disbelieve him. His face did look drawn, his eyes tired. "So when?"

"Maybe tomorrow." He got to his feet and collected the dishes. "Right now I'm going down to the river to wash these and collect some more water. Then I think I'll take a little nap. I've rigged up a small perimeter alarm system, so it should be safe enough if you don't start wandering around and trip the damn thing."

Tempest relaxed at the comment, feeling a return to their old footing. "I'll probably be asleep when you get back." She closed her eyes and missed the glint of satisfaction that flickered in his gaze before he turned from her.

"Mr. Whitney-King on line one, Josh." Josh frowned, glancing up from the report he'd been reading to stare at the interoffice link that carried the voice of his secretary.

"All right, I'll take it." He punched the correct number on his phone. "Yes, Arthur." Arthur called every day, sharing the lack of information and the worry.

"Have you heard from Stryker?"

"No. Greg checked in early this morning and said there was still no contact."

Arthur Whitney-King sighed roughly, worried in ways he hadn't been in years, ten to be exact, from the day he had handed over the responsibility of Tempest to Stryker. "It's been three days since he was dropped off two miles from the campsite." He sighed again, using his free hand to tap restlessly on the shiny black surface of his desk. "By the way, thanks for sending your plane down there with him. My pilot says yours is one of the best. If it gets bad, it may be the edge that gets them out alive."

"Thinking like that won't help anyone," Josh said sharply.

"Tell me about it. I run a multimillion-dollar empire but my daughter is stuck in some godforsaken corner of a rat hole, in who knows what kind of condition and under what specific circumstances, and I have to sit here waiting for word. She could be dead or worse. As could Stryker."

There wasn't much comfort to be had in the circumstances but Josh did his best. "He's a good man."

"Damn good with her. Better than the rest of us." His hand closed into a fist, which he slammed into the desk with enough force to hurt. "Damn, I wish I understood what drives her to this kind of thing. I love her in spite of the crazy stunts she pulls. We all do. I just wish she'd settle down. Marry someone, anyone, and live a normal life."

Josh listened to the unguarded words from a man who, by most accounts and his own observation, rarely discussed his personal life with his professional associates. "What's normal?" he murmured, thinking of his own rather unusual existence.

"Not trying to kill yourself is one good indicator," Arthur returned irritably. "If it weren't for the other two turning out all right, I'd wonder if I hadn't failed as a parent."

Josh could understand his feelings but there was little he could say to help. Instead, he stayed with the facts. "Greg's staying on top of the situation and Slater's sending a team down there this morning."

"I know. He called me. Thought for a while he was going to try to go himself."

Josh frowned deeply at the comment. Slater hadn't indicated anything of that nature to him. Of course, he knew better than Arthur just how serious Slater's injuries had been earlier in the year. He also knew that although Slater had healed, he was far from strong enough to attempt a rescue of the kind that Stryker might need.

"Look, I'm sorry I bothered you. I appreciate everything you're doing. And Stryker's brother."

"I know, Arthur. I'll keep you posted."

"Thanks, Josh. Right now, it's all that is keeping any of us here sane."

Josh listened to the dial tone a moment before he punched in Slater's number. His office answered on the first ring. A few seconds later he was speaking to Slater himself. "What's this I hear about you thinking of going to Central America yourself?" he demanded without preamble.

"Wishful thinking, damn it," Slater admitted with a rough growl of frustration and impatience. "As it is, I've yanked my best people from all over the place. Four of them, counting a pilot, are already on their way."

"I keep telling myself that we're all worrying needlessly. Your brother's good."

"Whether he's good or not, I need that team down there for my own peace of mind. Less than an hour ago, I heard that the rebels are heading back toward the river and this time they aren't moving in small guerrilla groups."

"Damn!"

"My feelings were a lot less printable."

"How far?"

"A day's hard march."

"Not much time."

"Got it in one."

"You think your people will be able to find them?"

"Two of them helped train Stryker and one helped with Tempest. If they're still alive, we'll find them."

Like Arthur, he demanded the same reassurance. "You'll keep me posted?"

"Bet on it."

FIVE

"I won't let you carry me." Tempest glared at Stryker's set face, her eyes flashing with the return of temper and energy that almost twenty-four hours of sleep had given her. She still felt rocky and her fever wasn't staying down completely but she wasn't about to burden Stryker with more problems than they already had. Night was setting around them, a dark cloak to conceal them from any would-be pursuers. She knew as well as he that to stay in one place for long was to court detection. She knew better than he what walking right now was going to cost her. Just this small display of emotion was ripping at her small reserve of strength.

While she was glaring at him, Stryker quelled his natural inclination to demand she listen to reason. Remembering all his plans and decisions, he chose a completely different line of attack. "All right." He went back to stuffing their meager belongings into his pack. The things she had collected from the relief camp were added to his stores.

"What do you mean, all right?" Tempest demanded suspiciously.

He shrugged, mentally congratulating himself on his course. For the first time he wasn't waging a pitched battle. He'd win. She wouldn't be able to walk far without help. And though Tempest was hide bent on her independence, she wasn't foolishly stupid. When her strength gave out, he'd carry her as he intended all along. And she'd accept, probably even apologize for being an ass, one of her favorite descriptions of herself when she made an error in judgment.

"Well?" she muttered, watching him, wondering at the ease with which he had agreed. Stryker never let her decide one thing. He always had a better way. Most of the time he was right, she acknowledged silently, but that didn't stop her from fighting with him about his choices.

Stryker shrugged into his pack. It was heavy but no weightier than it had been two days before. "I mean you can walk if you like. Frankly, I wasn't looking forward to carrying you anyway. This damn thing isn't light. And neither are you even if you are skinnier than I've ever seen you." That earned him a lethal look that should have dropped him in his tracks. "You want the point or shall I take it?"

She ignored that to peer up at him in the gathering gloom. "Are you feeling okay?"

"Yes." His lips twisted in faint amusement at her skepticism.

"You never give in to me."

Pulling on the infrared glasses, he led the way out of the clearing. She followed, not even realizing that she had. "Old tactics. New game." His voice was low, little more than a whisper below the level of the jungle coming alive for its nocturnal inhabitants.

Tempest was no less quiet. "Meaning?"

"Nothing dramatic. Just that I don't want to fight with you. I don't have the extra energy for one thing. And neither do you. All I want to do is get out of this mess, into a clean bed after an hour-long hot shower."

"Make that two," Tempest muttered, wiping her hand across her sweaty brow. They hadn't even made a quarter of a mile yet and she felt as though she had been on the move for hours. Sweat was pouring off her and her hands were shaking. At least Stryker was in front of her and wouldn't notice right away.

Stryker heard her labored breathing, silently cursing her pride. He could force her to obey him but they would pay a price that he didn't want to demand of either of them. So he waited, slowing his pace to a crawl, giving her every break he could. She managed a mile, the last few feet of it nearly breaking his resolve.

"Let's take a breather." He stopped, bracing himself instinctively as she plowed into his back. He caught her before she could go to her knees, lifting her into his arms and carrying her to a rock about ten feet away. He sat down, still holding her. "I've got you," he murmured, settling her comfortably against him. He snagged the canteen and uncapped it. Tipping it against her lips, he gave her two sips.

"Sorry," she breathed heavily, struggling to pull

herself together. "You were right. I was an ass."
His scent was sweat, pure Stryker and jungle. Nothing had ever smelled so good or so real.

"A pretty ass."

She lifted her head. "Don't be kind to me. I don't deserve it. Besides, only a blind man would see anything pretty about the way I am right now."

He brushed a kiss on the tip of her damp nose. "Then I must be blind. Your eyes are sleepy, a lot like they look just after we make love. You're soft in my arms."

Charmed when she shouldn't have been, touched when she had hoped she was finally over him, she mentally shied from the sensual web of words he was weaving. "And I look like I came through a bush on the tail of a hurricane."

He laughed, hugging her to him. "That too. But you wear it well." He kissed her again, taking his time, needing some kind of a reward for letting her choose her own way this time.

Tempest curled her arms around his neck and let his mouth reprint every sensation of his possession on her starving mind. He was heat held in check, passion hovering on the edge of release, and tenderness so gentle and rich that she wanted to curl into his arms and forget the world that beckoned like an impatient lover. His taste was vintage wine, silky smooth with a kick so subtly disguised that only a fool took more than a sip at a time. For this moment, she was a fool. It had been so long, a lifetime of waiting and wishing. For the first time, Stryker was seeing her as she was, trying to accept her independence. She knew he could have forced her to accept his help or even made her stay another day in the clearing. But he hadn't. He had let her find her way, walking with her, not pushing her, not demanding what she could give no one. When he raised his head to look into her eyes, her hand cupped his lean jaw.

"You want me." He allowed none of his surprise to show.

"Yes."

"How long?"

"Forever. An instant." She smiled faintly, her truth so well accepted that she found no difficulty in sharing it with him.

"Then why haven't you shown me? You're never shy about demanding what you want?"

She closed her eyes, hearing anger that hadn't been there a second before. "Demand? I don't demand anything of anyone. I can't. I know what that means in loss of pride, of dignity, or right of choice." She opened her lashes to watch him, praying that this time in this ill-chosen place, he would really hear what she had never had the courage to say. "I will not steal your freedom by chaining you with my needs, my wants, my hopes. It would be like caging your soul. So very wrong. So impossible to live with for either of us."

Stryker stared into her eyes, seeing the first candle of knowledge lit in the darkness of his conceptions of the woman he had seen grow from child to his Tempest. His great plan suddenly seemed the worst of masculine manipulation and arrogance. For the first time in his life he was ashamed of himself. He touched her lips, tracing their tender curve, glad at least he hadn't done more than just maneuver her over whether she would walk or not. He needed to think, to reassess, to shift his ideas into reality and truth.

"We need to go."

"I know."

He rose, her slight weight more dear to him than he would have admitted. "Try to sleep if you can."

She leaned her head on his shoulder and looped her arms around his neck. "I wish I could make it easier on you."

He kissed her gently, cherishing her in a way that was new to both of them. "Maybe you have," he whispered soundlessly above her head.

The journey in the darkness was slow, the heat of the day still hovering to make movement an effort. Stryker kept a steady pace, resting every forty-five minutes for fifteen. Tempest slept during the march, rousing slightly when he took a break but never coming awake completely. By the time dawn crawled across the sky, he had found a campsite and begun the task of hiding them from any unfriendly eyes.

Tempest stirred in the nest of blankets and soft limbs that he had used to make her bed. She stretched, feeling stronger than she had the day before, but still not as strong as she should have been. "You look tired," she murmured softly, coming to her knees beside him as he unpacked some food from the pack. "Let me do that while you relax." She touched his arm, stilling his movements.

Stryker looked at her, seeing a hint of color in her pale cheeks. Her eyes were brighter than they had been since he had found her. He touched her forehead, checking for fever. She was faintly warm. The fever was still hanging on. Worried but determined not to show it, he asked, "How do you feel?"

She grinned, wanting to see the clouds of concern leave his eyes. "Hungry."

His lips twitched at the immediate reply. Tempest was five feet two and had the appetite of a field hand. "That bad, huh?"

"Got it in one." She pulled the pack out of his grasp and started rummaging through the contents. There wasn't a huge selection of freeze-dried ingredients but there was enough to stave off hunger. "How do you feel about stew for breakfast?"

Sitting back on his heels, Stryker watched her, realizing something that he had always taken for granted. Tempest, unlike any other woman of his acquaintance, had an ability to take anything that life dished out and still make the most of her serving. She didn't complain when it really mattered; she didn't whimper, run, or hide. She faced life on its own terms and then found a way to live fully and completely in the moment.

Tempest lifted her head, her eyes curious at his slow reply. "Are you still in there?" she teased, holding three packets of vegetables and meat aloft.

"I'll get the water."

She shook her head. "No way. You did the donkey work. Now I'll pretend to be a chef and that includes getting the water. I can hear the river, so we can't be far." She poked a finger into the hard wall of his chest. "You rest. It's my turn to work." She waited, positive he would refuse to let her help but equally positive that in the end she would do just as she intended.

Stryker saw that she was braced for battle. Suddenly, he grinned. She had always had that damn-your-eyes and full-speed-ahead kind of glare when she had winning as her goal. "All right."

She blinked, staring at him as though he had just grown three heads and a tail. Stryker never gave in without a fight and this was the second time in less than a day. "Are you sure you're all right?" This time it was her hand on his forehead checking for a fever.

He laughed, genuinely amused and enjoying himself in spite of the circumstances. "Yes."

"You don't have a fever. Do you feel sick?"

"No."

"Hit your head?"

"No."

"Dizzy from the heat?"

"No." He was dizzy all right but the heat had nothing to do with it. His emotions were born in the hot fire of holding Tempest in his arms, of seeing her eyes glow with concern, of learning her secrets, of finally seeing past her strength to a little of the vulnerability that she hid so well.

"Well, something sure is wrong," she muttered, eyeing him closely.

"Why?"

"That's the second time you've let me get my way."

He had opted for honesty, no longer intending to manipulate her into seeing what they could have together. He wanted her fairly. He would fight for her, with her, but never against her. "Maybe I'm learning."

"What?"

He shrugged, wondering why he had never thought to share with her instead of assert himself over her. "Things." Her curiosity was as bright and avid as her enthusiasm. He wanted it as well as her glorious body. He wanted her to look at her present, her past, and her future. He wanted the answers that they both would find there.

"What kind of things?"

"Cabbages and kings."

"I hate it when you get cryptic."

He nodded toward the packets she appeared to have forgotten she was holding. "I thought you were going to cook. I passed the point of hunger hours ago. I'm into starvation now. And there is a hell of a lot more of me to feed than you." He rolled smoothly off his knees and into a sitting position, using her bed as a couch and the trees lined behind it as a backrest. "Get to it, woman. Feed me. I've earned my keep. It's your turn."

She popped to her feet, playing it as lightly as he. "As you command, oh great carrier of poor, weak me."

His laugh followed her out of the small haven he had created in the jungle. The moment he couldn't see her, her pace slowed, her thoughts slipping into high gear.

Tempest felt as though the world had just changed its direction of rotation. Her life had been measured in the years before Stryker and those after. He was her friend, her rescuer, her onetime lover, and the man she had loved so long that it seemed as though she had always loved him. He didn't love her. She knew that, had accepted it when she had given him her virginity. She had understood that he didn't like her way of life, approve of her choices or even of her personality. But he had wanted her. She had thought it was enough. Like the eager child she had been at twenty, she had grasped his desire and let him teach her the rites between a man and a woman. The cost had been high. She had soared on the wings of passion in a flight she had never duplicated. He had marked her so completely his that no man then or since had touched her. So she roamed the world, more restless, more searching than before. The risks she took grew greater, but no matter how high or how far she flew, Stryker was always there waiting to catch her. Stryker was her constant, the axis around which she rotated, the sun in her sky, the wind beneath the wings of her freedom. As long as he existed in the world, she was safe.

But now the rules seemed to be changing between them. He was different. Still tough, still competent, and yet softer, almost tender with her. She frowned as she filled the pot she had brought for water. Stryker was never tender. And he never walked away from a fight with her.

"You look like you have the weight of the world on your shoulders. Stop worrying. By my reckoning we should make the city early tomorrow."

Tempest glanced up, startled. She hadn't even realized she had returned to camp. "I wasn't thinking of that," she admitted quietly.

"Then what?" he asked just as quietly.

She settled the pot over the small smokeless fire

Stryker had made while she was at the river. "Us. You and me."

He folded his arms across his chest, waiting for the next installment.

Tempest glanced at him and then away, for the first time in her dealings with Stryker feeling almost shy. "You're different."

"So are you."

At that she looked fully at him. "How?"

"More peaceful."

Her eyes widened. "Me?"

His smile was as gentle as his voice. "You didn't know?" He ached to touch her but he kept his hands firmly laced over his chest.

"No." She tipped her head, thinking about what he said. Stryker knew her well. He didn't understand her but he certainly was observant where her behavior was concerned. She had to take his word for it. "What makes you think so?"

"For one thing you aren't fidgeting like you should be by now. You're on the mend, getting your energy back. But look at you. You're sitting there quietly. No finger tapping, no urgent need to be up and away. Peaceful."

"I've been sick," she defended herself, wondering why she felt as though he were insulting her when she knew very well the opposite was true.

"That wouldn't have stopped you a year ago. Remember the broken leg that you were supposed to rest. Remember the wheelchair race and throwing yourself into that damn hedge."

She grimaced. She could still hear his curse in her sleep and recall exactly how gently he had pulled her out of the bushes and held her horrified and exasperated family at bay. "I admitted that wasn't very smart but I was bored."

"You had just gotten out of the hospital that day. You didn't even know exactly how that mechanical marvel you insisted on worked. That damn driveway wasn't banked for Indy type driving," he said flatly.

She shrugged, feeling the strangest need to apologize. "I'm sorry." The words popped out, surprising them both.

Stryker's eyes narrowed at the guilty look he had never seen on her face.

"It was a stupid thing to do. Everyone was frantic."

"You scared us all. I looked out Arthur's study window and saw you flying down the concrete like a suicidal pilot."

She leaned forward, resting her weight on his arms as she brushed his lips with hers. Tears stood in her eyes, brightening the blue as sunlight against a clear sky. "I didn't mean to do that. I didn't think."

He breathed in her scent and the jungle that added a primitive earthiness to her fragrance. He stared into her eyes, feeling the shock of her tears go straight past every defense he had ever built against her. He could match her strength and win but her softness, this sudden gentleness and contrition, was beyond his power to combat. He unfolded his arms. Tempest lost her balance and tumbled against his chest. He caught her close, raising her chin with one hand as he cupped the nape of her neck with the other.

"Do you have any idea how often in the last four

years I reached out for you in the darkness and came up empty?''

''No?'' she whispered, searching the features she could have drawn blind.

''A thousand. A million.''

''There have been other women.'' She hated knowing that someone else had shared his nights, known his passion, his desire. She had been unable to find pleasure or relief with anyone else. At times, she almost hated him for that.

Stryker didn't deny it, although, in that moment, he wished he could. ''They weren't you.''

''They were someone.'' She closed her eyes, appalled she had betrayed that.

Stryker stared at her, reading the knowledge that burned like a hot poker in his gut. When they had parted, he had done his best to forget her and to remember that she had a right to share her bed and life with any man she chose. Just because she had given him her virginity meant no more than he had been the first. It gave him no special rights, no privileges.

''Why?'' His thumb traced the outline of her lips. ''You're a beautiful woman built for loving. You're generous with your passion. You gave me more in those few days than I have ever had in my life.'' When she neither looked at him nor answered with another explanation, a more painful one presented itself. ''Did I hurt you in some way that I don't know? Honey, I never meant it. Don't you know I would rather be tortured to a slow death than hurt you in any way?''

Tempest opened her eyes, reading the pain in his.

He had hurt her but not in the way that he meant or that she dared explain. "Lovemaking with you was all that I imagined and more." That much she could give him. "You made me feel special and beautiful and most desired. I loved it." She touched his mouth, those lips that had taught her about pleasure and her own body. Words had brushed her skin with every kiss he had traced along her length. He had told her things that still stopped her breath just with their memory. He had worshiped her body with his touch, breaching the barrier of innocence with such gentleness that she had known no pain, only exquisite sensation without end.

"But there was no other after me." A fact that was written forever in his mind.

Her eyes, usually so clear, so full of emotion and thought, were mirrors reflecting nothing but the image of his own confusion. "No."

Stryker had the feeling that Tempest had just handed him one of the keys he sought but he didn't know where or how it fit in the whole. Clearly, she wouldn't tell even if she knew. Problems, he was good at solving them he reminded himself. Think. He touched her lips again, watching her eyes darken with desire. He could feel his own body tighten, his memory supplying the images of her naked in his arms. He brought her mouth close, breathing the same air as she. "When this is over, will you come to me?"

The hardest word she had ever said. "No."

"You want me."

She would not lie. "Yes."

"You won't let me love you."

"You don't love me. You desire me as you desired those before me and those who will come after." She brushed his lips, her tongue tracing the contours, relearning the taste she had never forgotten nor exorcised. "I enter no man's harem. Not even yours."

SIX

Stryker took her mouth even as her words slipped into his mind, to lodge there, to grow, to demand answers he didn't have but would find. He molded her to him, feeling as though he were bringing her home where she belonged. His kiss deepened and she allowed it, meeting him, matching his passion and his need. Her moan of pleasure was softer but no less telling than his own. He stroked her back, pressing her hips against his, letting her feel the strength of her power over him. When he raised his head to look at her, her lashes were closed, her arms around his neck, her body arched over his arm.

"Look at me."

Tempest opened her eyes.

"You are not nor have you ever been part of my harem." His voice was husky with restraint but sharp enough to slice away any attempt at a man's evasion to satisfy himself at a woman's expense. "You are special to me. That isn't a phrase. It's my truth for you. There is no other Tempest in my life nor will there ever be. Wherever you or I go, whatever you or I do, we are part of each other. Maybe it isn't love. I know damn well it isn't liking either. Neither of us is tepid enough for that word anyway. What I feel for you doesn't have a name but it's too damn strong to die even when I tried to kill it in the arms of other women. Hate me for that if you must but it won't change one thing between us.''

"I couldn't hate you if I tried.''

"Then take what we can have together.''

"We tried that and it didn't work.''

Both remembered the joy and the pain.

"We're older.''

"Less likely to bend.''

He laughed at that. "You've never bent for anyone or anything in your life.'' There was no sarcasm in his reply, only honesty.

"Neither have you.''

He thought a moment, wanting to have her any way that she would allow, needing her in ways that had just grown stronger with the years. "We could try.''

Tempest searched his eyes, reading his need, knowing its depth matched her own. "And if we did?'

"Are you asking for guarantees?''

"No, life doesn't come with them. We both know that.''

"Then what is it that you want from me?''

"I need to know where we're heading, that we're trying for something more than an open-ended arrangement that means nothing more than an agreement to share a bed.''

To say he was startled if not amazed would have been understating the situation. ''You, who would risk your life on a whim without ever looking an inch ahead of your nose, are afraid to take a leap into my arms, a place you've been before?'' He touched her face, tilting her head so that he could look deeply into her eyes. ''What is it that you aren't telling me?''

Tempest tried to brazen it out but there was just so much lying a woman could do when held in a man's arms, her body cradled intimately against his.

Stryker inhaled sharply, his gaze narrowing on the soft flush that tinted her skin, the lashes that fluttered with nervousness that was as alien to Tempest as the shocking realization that was forcing its way into his mind. ''How long?'' he demanded hoarsely.

''How long what?'' She pushed against his shoulders, squirming for release. She didn't get it or the distance that might have helped disguise her emotions.

''How long have you loved me?''

''I didn't say that I did.'' She pushed harder, swearing when he simply gathered her impossibly closer.

''You wouldn't have. I freely admit I don't understand a lot about you but I know damn well you wouldn't have told me that you loved me if you hadn't felt the feelings were reciprocated. I've never known you to demand anything emotionally from anyone, least of all me.'' Using one arm to trap her straining body against his chest, he wrapped his hand around her throat, stroking the slender length in soothing sweeps. But there was no succor from his too accurate memories. ''I hurt you that afternoon when I pulled you out of that tree.'' His conclusion was no question, no reasoning with a loophole for escape. ''You stood there and agreed to call it a day without any sign of regret. Do you know how often in the last four years I've wondered if teaching you about sex wasn't just one more lesson you had maneuvered me into giving you?''

Appalled, Tempest covered his mouth with her hand. ''No. It was never like that.''

He kissed her palm, touching his tongue to the center. Her shiver of response went through him with the finesse and power of a stiletto. ''I don't know what to say to you,'' he murmured against her flesh. ''I wish I could tell you I felt the same way.''

Her smile was sad and accepting. ''But you don't. I knew it then. I know it now. But can't you see, that's why I can't lie with you. I, too, tried to kill what I feel. I couldn't run far enough or fast enough to do it. It's crammed into my heart and mind so completely that wherever I went, whatever I did, you were there, whether it was in my dreams or nightmares or when you had to pull me out of some mess.''

''Marry me.'' The words slipped out, stunning them both.

''No.'' She had thought she was intimately acquainted with pain, but she discovered that it was only a forerunner of the agony of his loveless proposal. She tried to push out of his arms.

Stryker grabbed her shoulders.

''You're crazy,'' she hissed, her voice broken,

shattered by the dream that was her worst nightmare. Bitterness she had never allowed to surface erupted. "I drive you nuts on a regular basis. You make a great nursemaid but I don't want to marry one. And I can't change. We both know that. And you would want me to and we both know that too. I can't be caged, even by love. My family have tried for years. Do you think I can't feel their resentment, irritation, frustration? Father sent you down here, offered you any help you needed just so that he could get the daughter he admits he doesn't understand but still loves anyway home where she'll be safe. Not that he expects me to stay there. God forbid. I'm a black sheep, shocking in this family of wunderkinds and wealth."

Stryker had wanted the keys to her thinking, her actions. In a few short seconds she had handed him the whole ring. She had her father pegged and her family. Every one of them loved her in spite of herself, just as he cared about her in spite of the hell she had put him through.

Tempest strived to calm herself. She didn't blame her family for what they couldn't give. "You remember Grandmother Tempest?"

"Yes."

"She loved me. Not because of my faults or in spite of them but she simply loved me. She was the least adventurous human being I've ever known but she loved me. Everyone has a secret wish in his heart. That's mine." Tears stood in her eyes, overflowed crystalline streams of sorrow for what would never be hers. "You want me but you hate what I am. How can I give myself to you knowing that? How can I survive when the giving turns to hate and bitter words and if-only-you'd-change demands?''

Slowly, knowing the truth of her words, seeing the personal clarity that he never would have credited her with possessing, Stryker released her. He hurt in ways he hadn't believed possible. He had never felt so helpless, so at a loss. He, who could solve the unsolvable, had no answer. Only sorrow, sadness, for her, for himself, for the future he wanted and would never have. For in spite of everything, the need even now sharpening its claws in his body, the desire that no woman but she could assuage, he knew he would not touch her again. ''I'm sorry.'' Words were as useless as regrets but they were all he could give her now.

''For what? We rarely can command ourselves to be more or less than we are.'' She shifted to her knees, needing distance between them. ''We are who we are. My love is my problem. Not yours.'' She glanced away from the eyes that saw her too well. She wanted to hide but she neither had the luxury of a place to go nor would she permit herself the indulgence. The water in the pot was boiling gently, ready for the stew ingredients. Her appetite was a poor thing but they both needed food. She moved closer to the fire and ripped open the first packet. She could feel Stryker watching her every move but he didn't speak and neither did she, not then nor later through the meal. When he finally broke the silence, she jumped. If he noticed, he gave no sign of it.

''How tired are you?''

''Not very.'' Not quite true but the idea of lying

with him in the bed he had made was a hell she wouldn't endure.

Stryker slid his gun across to her and then lay down on the pallet on his back. "How about keeping watch for a while? Give me three hours, then I'll take over."

She nodded as she checked the weapon and angled herself on the rock on which she was sitting so that she could see the main points of entry to their camp. Her senses tuned to the jungle, she still heard the sounds of Stryker settling in. They stood out in the small animal noises, teasing her with what could never be. Marriage. He had caught her unawares with that reaction. In all her thinking, somehow she had always assumed they'd never get that far. She sighed deeply, wishing she could be what he needed and could really love, wishing she could throw off this yoke of restlessness that made her a prisoner of her own impulses. Why couldn't she be like other women, content with their routine lives or at least responsible with their chance taking? Of all the answers she sought, this one had eluded her the longest and the most completely.

Stryker needed sleep. His whole body felt the weight of the demands he had placed on it. But Tempest's revelations had been too shocking, too impossible for him to forget or even to accept without examining every word. She loved him. How could he have been so blind? He had known there were a hundred veils of mystery to her thinking, her actions but he would have bet his last penny that he could have recognized her emotions. They were so clear, so generous, so honest. But she had hidden herself from him. Even now he felt the betrayal of that realization. Yet, had he the right to feel anything? She had protected herself and him in the only ways open to her. Generous. One of her greatest and most endearing traits. She gave to others always before herself.

He thought of the grandmother she spoke of with such affection. The older Tempest had been a gentle woman, soft in the ways of the old version of femininity. She had been married young to a man who had ruled her home and person with strength rather than understanding. And yet, out of that environment, she had been able to touch her namesake with more kindness and awareness of the younger Tempest's needs than any of her contemporaries or her family. She truly had loved Tempest. No conditions, no demands for change, nothing but untainted, free love.

He thought of himself, the times his heart had been in his throat over one of her escapades. He had shouted, raved at her, losing a temper he never allowed to surface except with her. Foolish, criminally stupid, crazy. He had called her all of those and more. He had often wanted to lock her up for her own good, knowing full well that any kind of confinement would have killed her spirit as surely as a well-placed knife could have stilled her heart. She was his cross, the thorn in his side, the woman he wanted beyond all others. They all carried full measures of angry caring, resentment, and frustration. He didn't want to face that about himself and the way he felt about her but he had to acknowledge the truth, for her sake and his own. Yet could he walk away from what little they could share as she so plainly intended that they should do?

His lashes closed against the filtered light of the sun shining through the trees overhead. He considered the question but could find no real answer. Either course would demand tremendous strength and desire, one for survival, the other for the woman. On that realization he let sleep take his thoughts and bring relief to his exhausted body. His decision would come, but this time he would make it with total knowledge of the woman he wanted and cared about but did not love.

"Have you heard from the team yet, Slater?" Josh demanded.

"They arrived this morning and met with your pilot. I just finished talking with Randy. He said the guerrillas seem to be between the camp and the city. He's not sure because most of the information he's been able to get this far is coming from talking with the natives fleeing out of the region rather than from the government. They've slammed a lid on almost everything going in or coming out. If it weren't for the fact that Whitney-King was involved, I doubt we'd have been permitted into the city at all."

Josh's dark eyes narrowed. "Greg says he has clearance to leave whenever Stryker gets back to the plane."

"That's still on. So far."

Josh swore once.

"I agree." Slater sighed roughly and raked his

fingers through his hair. "I feel so damn helpless sitting up here."

"Don't play the fool. You aren't up to the kind of demands that terrain would make and you know it. Stryker's no fool. He'll get her out if it's at all possible. And the team you sent down there may be able to contact him, and if not, at least they'll be backup if he needs help."

"They aren't going to do much good if we don't hear something soon. We don't even know if he's found Tempest or even if she's still alive."

"I wish Joe could get a fix on them for us."

Slater sat up straighter. In his anxiety over his brother he had forgotten about Josh's paranormal brother. "You asked him?"

"He got only one thing. He's fairly certain the two of them are together."

Slater slouched back in his chair. "That's something at least."

"Damn little."

Slater sighed deeply. "I'll call you if I have any word."

"Likewise."

"I told you to wake me," Stryker said angrily as he rolled to his feet and glared at the sun that was slowly sinking into night.

Tempest looked around from the pot she was stirring over the fire. "You needed the rest." She shrugged, ignoring the temper she had expected. "I took my antibiotic on schedule and now I'm fixing supper. I haven't seen or heard anyone or anything unusual all day."

Stryker studied her, remnants of his deep sleep slowing his emotional reflexes. He watched the sunset dance in her hair, traced the flush from the heat of the cook fire that so reminded him of those moments of passionate abandon they had shared. His body tightened, re-creating even more images, physical responses of the time that she had decreed would never come again. He clenched his fists against the denial screaming in his mind as he tried to concentrate on the argument. "You still should have called me. You need sleep more than I do."

"I'm going to take a nap right after we eat. You even get to clean up. Does that make you feel any better?"

The calm way she returned his irritation was a flame thrower to the desire burning in him. Before he could stop himself, before he could remember all her reasons and his own, he reached for her, her mouth, her body, any part of her he could hold for as long as she would allow. He expected a fight and received compliance so swift, so consuming that any lingering hints of reason died a final death. As he took her lips, her arm encircled his neck, her other hand trapped between them.

His kiss was hot, fire in the heat of the jungle. His hands sculpted her body to his, demanding her surrender and offering his own. Tempest met his passion, taking what he gave and demanding more yet again. She had watched him sleep, standing guard over him as he had for her. Knowing that he would have trusted few people to that extent was the first crack in her resolve. The long hours of thinking of an empty future was the second. She was a survivor.

She could take what he could give her for as long as he would give it and make it enough.

Stryker felt the raging need and fought his own primordial urge to claim the woman he knew belonged to him by choice and his own claiming. He raised his head, his hand going to the buttons of her blouse. If he had not looked into her eyes, he wouldn't have remembered that she loved him. The knowledge went through him, stopping him as nothing else would have done.

"Damn you, why? You said that you didn't want this but you aren't just letting me have you, you're demanding I take you."

"I know."

"Another risk?" Anger at her and himself sharpened his voice.

"No. I want you. You want me. The rest is only my problem. Not yours."

"Like hell." His hand lay heavy against her breast just above her heart. The steady beat reminded him of how precious her life was, how close, so many times, he had come to losing her.

Tempest pressed his fingers into her skin, her body quickening at the caress they both wanted and he was too stubborn to take. "I won't ask for more than you can give."

"I want to give you marriage. You won't take that."

She unfastened the buttons herself, sliding his hand against her breast, feeling it sigh into the palm of his hand. "But I will give you this. You said we could try compromising. This is mine."

His thumb and forefinger teased her nipple. Her

eyes darkened in response. And still he watched her, trying to understand, knowing that he had to or he would lose something he would never regain. "I care about you," he groaned, dipping his head to trace her lips.

Her fingers threaded through his hair, holding him close. "I know. You may rave at me for getting into a fix but it has always been you who taught me how not to make the same mistakes again. I owe you my life so many times over."

"I don't want your gratitude," he breathed against her skin as he measured the length of her throat to the smooth flesh below.

"I know. Some things between us are more than words." She gasped softly as his mouth took her nipple, sucking lightly at the taut bud, tenderly skimming the dusky circle around it until her body arched in supplication for more.

"I shouldn't do this."

"If you don't, I'll take you instead," she breathed roughly, her fingers pulling at his shirt until his chest was bare. "Four long years of loneliness. I need you." She lifted to him, pressing her aching breasts into the warmth of the pelt that shielded the solid wall of muscles that held her so carefully, so safely through the long night march.

"There was never a day I didn't think of you." He pushed her shirt from her shoulders, his gaze lingering on every bruise, every small scar and blemish of the life she had chosen. So much courage in one small body. His grip tightened, a futile effort to protect that was as reflexive and involuntary as his breathing.

Her lashes half closed, she studied his passion-drawn features. Stryker was too strongly defined to be handsome but for her there was no man to match him in looks. "Then stop talking now. The night won't wait for us."

He laughed softly, knowing no other woman who could command in that husky little voice, look serious enough to run him through if he didn't obey while all the while her body was warm and waiting for his touch, her lips tender from his kisses and her arms strong and sure chaining him to her side. "No, it won't wait and neither will you." He pulled her belt loose from her shorts and pushed them down her legs in two smooth strokes. "Good thing you left off the boots."

Tempest was busy with her own valet service. She stopped long enough to grin. "Same for you." A second later he was as nude as she. Neither spoke for a moment, both looking at the other, making no secret of the pleasure they found in their chosen mates. When he pulled her close, she wrapped herself around him. His hands traced her curves, the secret places that had ached for his loving. Moisture shone on their skin, gilded gold by the setting sun. Her moans of delight were soft, mere whispers of sounds. His gasps of pleasure were husky, clear on the soft breeze that suddenly blessed the land. As he rose above her, his arms taking his weight, he stared into her eyes. She watched him as he entered slowly, sinking into her body and deeper into her heart with the care and the reverence of her after so long a drought of loving.

"All right?" he demanded, stopping halfway. Although it felt as though his body were being drawn on a rack, he would not hurt her for his desire to make her his once more.

"Yes." She arched up against him, pulling him into her for his final thrust home. "Oh, yes," she breathed, her hips taking up the rhythm they had been too long denied.

Stryker closed his eyes, his need so fierce that to look at her would court insanity. He matched her pace, parrying every move, thinking of her joy and his fulfillment. But it was too quick in coming, the heat too intense to be slowed. He tried, grabbing her hips, holding her close. She would have none of it. She dug her nails into his back, whispering promises that threw him over the ridge before he realized he was balanced too close to the ultimate free-fall. Her cry of completion was a split instant behind his. The jungle listened, silent, waiting, knowing that once more man had mated with woman there in the wild, a piece of the Garden of Eden where all life had begun.

SEVEN

Stryker started to lift off Tempest.

Her arms tightened around him. "No, stay."

"I'm too heavy." He rolled over, bringing her with him so that she lay on his chest.

"Not to me." She raised her head to smile at him.

Stryker stared at that smile, knowing Adam must have looked at one just like it and known the urge to give birth to the human race. "No regrets?" He tucked a wayward curl behind her ear, his fingers lingering over the small whorled shape, tracing it, gently thrusting at the tiny hole.

She nipped his neck, licking the salt from his skin, getting high on his scent as it suffused every breath she took. "Not one," she whispered.

"If you married me, we could do this a lot." He slid his hands down her back, cupping her bottom.

"I'd drive you crazy in a week."

"Then we'd fight and make up." He pulled her

111

closer into the cradle of his hips, nudging her, reminding her of the magic they made when they came together. "The making up would make it worthwhile."

"No, it wouldn't." She covered his lips, wondering why he kept pushing for marriage and knowing that just this once she lacked courage, courage enough to ask, to seek this one answer.

Stryker let her taste fill his senses even as he allowed her body to ease the need that was beginning to build again. He hadn't lost yet. The more she fought, the more she evaded, the more determined he was that she see what they could have. He had no illusions. Tempest wasn't a woman who lived in a make-believe world. She would drive him crazy. And he would yell and swear. And try to protect her from herself. But he would never, ever cage her. And that one fact was, he was certain, what was keeping her from accepting his proposal. No, he wasn't fool enough to love her. He had seen what that meant and did to her family. But he would care for her, closer than ever, more completely, and irrefutably.

"Are you sure you don't want me to carry you?" Stryker demanded in a soft whisper that didn't carry more than a foot in the darkness. "You never did get your nap."

Tempest kept her hands twisted in the lead he had made for her. With only one pair of night glasses, he was the sighted one of them. "I'm fine. But we'd make better time if you'd stop checking on me every five steps," she murmured, smiling a little at the oath he muttered. "I'll squeak when I give out."

"Your word?" Before she could answer, Stryker stopped short, slipping into the brush to their right with almost no sound. He covered her lips with his hand, signaling her silence.

Tempest froze, straining her ears to detect the reason for Stryker's grab for cover. Then she heard them, voices, male, Spanish, which she understood. The rebels. Setting up camp. Obeying the pressure of Stryker's hand, she sank down, pressing into the dirt and the litter of the fallen limbs and leaves. His body was warm and solid next to her, a human barrier between her and danger. She felt him draw his gun, knew that he would protect her with his life. Her fingers tightened around the rifle she had taken from one of the fallen men at the encampment and that, until now, Stryker had been carrying for her. Along with her lessons in primitive survival at Stryker's insistence, she had learned to handle firearms during Slater's course. She wasn't as good as Stryker but she'd make hurting her or the man she loved costly.

Stryker counted heads. Fifteen. Rotten odds by any standard and the band was digging in for the night right in their path. They didn't dare try to withdraw. One startled animal sound or a breaking branch at the wrong moment and he and Tempest would be caught. The night glasses gave him an edge, but it did damn little for Tempest if he went down or they got separated. Leaning close to her ear, he mouthed, "We stay."

She squeezed his fingers to signal her understanding. Like Stryker, she had read the situation and realized as hard as it was their best chance lay in staying put. The thick foliage around them was cover night or day. And nothing she heard so far indicated that the group was searching for anyone in particular, which meant that although they would stay alert, they weren't turning over every leaf. With luck, the camp would break with the morning and they could be on their way as soon as the rebels passed.

It was a long, tedious night. Tempest slept in snatches, her hand wrapped around her rifle. She knew Stryker hadn't closed his eyes once. The posted sentries had passed them at regular intervals but not so near that their danger was appreciably increased. Dawn crept across the heavens in a cloak of silver, blue, and pink. The rebels awoke with grunts and grumbles. The coffee smelled too good and the food they cooked over the open fire even better. Tempest glanced at Stryker, signing her hunger and disgust at their pinned-down position. His lips twitched as he silently returned the same feeling. But neither moved. Finally, less than an hour later, the group packed up. Tempest and Stryker stayed hidden for another hour just in case there was a rear guard they hadn't seen.

"Looks like we can get out of here," Stryker muttered, easing out of the brush while keeping watch. Tempest was equally alert as she rose to her feet beside him. "What now? Camp or push on?" She would have liked nothing better than to sleep for hours on end. Her fever was building again, sapping her strength. It wouldn't be long before Stryker noticed.

"I don't like the risk but we'd better push on. We should be able to make the city today." He divided his glance with her and the narrow path they had been following.

Tempest bent down as though to retie her boot. She didn't dare face his complete scrutiny. They had to move on. The risk of stopping or slowing was too great when they were this close to getting to the city.

"Can you do it? It will be harder going in the heat."

"I'll make it," she murmured, making her voice more confident than she felt. She rose and tucked her rifle under one arm, ready for use if necessary but otherwise comfortable for walking. "You lead. I'll bring up the rear. If I can't take the pace, I'll tell you. I promise." With any luck he'd put any heightened color down to her change in position rather than fever. Mentally, she crossed her fingers as she gestured to the trail.

Stryker caught the back of her neck, yanked her close, and kissed her hard. "If I've got to be in this damn jungle with nuts running around trying to kill me, I'm glad I'm with you." He released her as quickly as he had taken her and turned to lead out, the need to get her to safety for once dulling his senses to the fire beginning to build in her body.

Tempest touched her tender lips, the yearning in her eyes so deep that Stryker would have won his battle in that moment if he had seen and followed up on his advantage.

Stryker set an easy pace in spite of what Tempest had told him. He wanted to put as much distance between them and the rebel band as possible, but he didn't want to use up Tempest's returning energy in a foolhardy forced march. At the first stop, only a half hour later, he prepared himself for her irritation at the slow trek. He wasn't prepared for what she did.

Tempest sat down on the fallen trunk in the minuscule clearing after checking for any unwanted inhabitants that might take exception to her making their home her couch. "Tell me you still have something in that pack that resembles food I can eat while I'm walking. I'm starved." She uncapped the canteen he passed her and drank carefully despite her raging thirst.

"This do?" He tossed a fruit and grain bar in her lap.

"Only if you've got two or three others in there and that doesn't mean giving me your share either. I'll swallow this snail's pace but I'm not taking your food." She didn't know where she was getting the energy to carry on this bravado but she intended to play the game as long as she could. With luck, her strength would hold to the city.

"I thought you'd get to that first," he said, grinning as he took out three more bars, kept two for himself, and handed her the other. "And for stopping so soon."

"Two or three years ago I would have. I was a royal pain. Still am if it comes to that, but I'm beginning to learn that I'm not indestructible. These days I try to behave sensibly." She took a healthy bite of her bar and forced it down her sore, dry throat. "Or at least for me I do," she amended fairly. "Besides, in this case, you would have been the one paying the price for my stupidity. That isn't fair."

Stryker studied her as he ate his own snack, disturbed by the brightness of her eyes and the pale flush on her cheeks. He reached out to touch her forehead, then froze as the sudden squawk of a startled bird brought every sense alert. He gestured for Tempest to hide in the brush behind their position. She rose swiftly, silently, and faded into the foliage, her rifle trained on the clearing. Stryker crowded beside her, his body between her and possible danger as they pressed close to the earth, ears straining for the slightest noise to indicate the threat, if any, and the direction. A twig snapped.

Tempest's fingers tightened on the rifle. Beside her, she felt Stryker's muscles ripple with tension and readiness. Then they were there. Three men, spread in a searching pattern, dressed in camouflage to blend with the green and brown of the jungle.

"I'll be damned," Stryker muttered softly against her ear. "Rescue."

At the moment he said the last word, Tempest recognized one of the men. Her grip on the rifle relaxed as she let her body lean against his for one instant of relief. He hugged her tightly.

Staying where he was, Stryker called quietly to the leader, the one most likely to know his voice. "Randy."

The three men swung around, guns at firing position, eyes scanning the clearing at the sound of Stryker's greeting. "Damn it, Stryker, are you trying to get yourself killed?" Randy demanded. "Your brother, John, would have our hides on his office wall."

"Try Slater, Randy, and I might believe you accept who I am." Stryker watched the older man absorb the correction and then gesture to his group that this meeting was no rebel trick. Stryker rose while signaling Tempest to stay down until he allowed Randy the precaution of a visual ID. He didn't want any accidents in the aftermath of the tense situation.

Randy lowered his gun while his companions spread out to keep watch. "You find her?"

Stryker turned, lifted his hand, and Tempest rose out of the foliage, her rifle tucked under her arm in a hold that brought a grin to Randy's lined face.

"Damn, girl, I'm glad to see you. That daddy of yours has been ripping up the phone lines between here and home. He's been on everyone's rear from the State Department to the janitor at the embassy."

Tempest grimaced, not even bothering with the futile wish her family would cease to bird-dog her like a single child in a houseful of adults. "Sorry he got you dragged down here for nothing. Stryker got me out."

"Yeah, well there is still a little matter of getting you the last twenty miles to the city. That's why we're here. You've got a group of nuts burning and raiding on this side of the river between you and your destination. We circled around from the south. Adds about twenty more miles but it's a lot safer."

Stryker swore graphically.

"Right." Randy grinned, his green eyes bright and clearly enjoying the bonus of fieldwork instead of training a bunch of amateurs in the art of survival. "After that it's a straight shot to the airfield. Our plane left this morning with the last bunch of Americans in the area. Josh's little baby, with an honor guard of five soldiers to keep the rebels honest, is standing ready on the runway with that hotshot Greg at the controls. The stories that man tells make me wish I had been with him when he learned his little tricks."

Stryker glanced at Tempest. "You ready?"

"I'm very ready for a shower with hot water and a clean bed I don't have to share with interesting creepy crawlies."

Randy tapped her on the back. "Always said you had guts, girl."

"I wish you'd stop calling me girl, boy."

He laughed. "Can't. Stryker would have my hide if I noticed you are built to give a man thoughts on pretty women and nights spent without talking."

He swung into the lead, waving his men to take up flanking positions. Tempest followed him and Stryker guarded her back. Tempest kept to the pace Randy set. It wasn't as easy as Stryker's but it was bearable. Their breaks were faster too, and when they finally veered away from the river, circling the line that the rebels had drawn between them and the city, she was beginning to feel the effects of the heat and the march. Sweat poured off her skin, trying to cool her heated flesh but only succeeding in making her feel as though she were wrapped in wet plastic film.

Stryker watched the smooth line of Tempest's back, the way her movements pushed over the trail rather than flowed with each step. She was laboring. Her shirt was wet, her arms glistening with moisture. She hadn't stumbled once but he knew it wouldn't be long. He cursed silently, then made his decision.

"Randy, break."

He stopped, turning quickly, his brows raised in

surprise. Stryker waved a hand at Tempest's wilting figure before she had a chance to turn around to see what he was doing.

Tempest knew she had never heard a sweeter word than that one. She let her rifle butt rest on the ground as she simply leaned against the base of a huge banana plant and closed her eyes. She couldn't go much farther and she hated admitting it and hated even more being a burden to the four men who had come after her.

"How do you want to handle it?"

"I'll carry her."

Tempest opened her eyes, wanting to argue, but one look at Stryker's face warned her that any protest was useless. She watched listlessly as he handed over his backpack to one of the flank men and his rifle to the other. He plucked her weapon out of her hands and gave it to Randy before lifting her in his arms. The moment her body settled against his, he felt the heat of her skin through the double thickness of their clothes. He stared at her face, cursing silently as he realized the flush he had taken as exertion was more. Fever. Out of control and fighting the medicine that at the very least should have taken the edge off the fire.

Tempest didn't see the anxiety in his eyes or his look at Randy as the older man, too, read the signs with concern. "I hate this," she muttered, relaxing against him and wrapping her arms around his neck to help him carry her more comfortably.

The two exchanged a look over her exhausted body. The pace would be a killer but there was no alternative now. "I know." He took his place behind Randy. "Let's go."

Randy murmured a word to his two companions, then set out. "We'll take her in quarter relays. Yell when you need relief."

"I will."

Tempest lost track of time. She was exhausted and couldn't keep her eyes open. She slept, waking fitfully only once, when she felt different arms hold her. She wanted to protest she didn't want another, any other man, caring for her. Only the knowledge of the physical cost to Stryker kept her silent. It wasn't until he took her back that she relaxed completely again, sleeping deeply, missing the concerned look he gave her as the day wore on and he could feel the fever continuing to build in spite of the heavier dose of antibiotics and aspirin.

"How bad?" Randy asked as they stopped for the final break before the last leg.

"At least a hundred and two."

"Unless someone's swiped our vehicle, we should be at the airfield in another two hours. We'll have her back in the US of A by morning." He studied Tempest as she lay curled against Stryker's chest with the complete trust of a much loved child. "Gutsy girl. Never heard a whimper out of her during the course. She's the kind of woman that makes a man proud."

"She also puts a man's heart in his throat more times than is safe."

Randy chuckled softly. "Better that than one of those whiny types that make you wish you could wring her neck." He started to reach out to touch her cheek, but one look at Stryker's hard eyes made him change his mind. "Hell, man, she's your woman. Anyone can see that. I was only checking that fever."

"Any checking and I'll do it."

He shrugged. "Can't say as I blame you." He rose, shouldering the extra gun. "You ready?"

Stryker nodded and came to his feet. "More than. I want to get her out of this hothouse and get this fever down. Those damn drugs aren't doing anything right."

"We're almost home."

"What do you mean you won't let us leave without Miss Whitney-King's passport?" Randy glared at the colonel standing in front of him. "You know who this woman is."

"I know nothing, señor. You say this is Señorita King. I do not know you and I have not met her. She has no papers. You cannot prove who she is," he repeated stubbornly. He spread his hands, his dark eyes implacable. "Without papers she does not leave."

The sun was fire hot, shining on the tableau. Stryker stood with a half-conscious Tempest in his arms. Randy's team flanked him. The soldiers watched them all. Randy and the colonel had been arguing for fifteen minutes without getting anywhere. Stryker's temper was almost as overheated as the landscape.

He stepped forward, his guards moving with him. "Colonel, this woman is burning up with fever. You have denied us the use of the building over there and you won't allow us to put her on board the plane to get her out of this heat. I know you have your orders. May we know what they are in regards to Miss King? What will you accept as identification?'' His professional life was a series of problems solved by any means. He had the expertise and the urgency of need to make this situation bend to his will.

The colonel turned to Stryker with relief, hearing no censure for the stand he had been ordered to take and only concern for the woman the man carried in his arms.

''If someone could be found who knows the señorita. Someone of our town, perhaps?''

''The only one who could have qualified on those grounds was the doctor at the relief center but she left on the last plane.''

The colonel's face furrowed with worry and a slowly awakening need to help. Belligerence hadn't won his cooperation but this man's determination and concern for his woman did. ''I cannot just allow you to leave.'' He spread his hands again. ''You must understand.''

Tempest stirred in Stryker's arms, muttering. ''Hot, Stryker.''

Stryker bent over her, shielding her with his body as much as he could. ''I know, baby. Just a while longer.''

''Wanna go home.''

Stryker stared into her fever-flushed face and came to a decision. It was a rare gamble but stranger things had occurred to him in the course of his life and paid off in the end. He raised his head, looking straight into the colonel's eyes. ''This is my woman, colonel. We are to be married when we get back to the States.

If you have a priest do it here and now, will that be enough?'' He glanced at Randy, ignoring his dumb-founded expression. ''My passport's in the left vest pocket. Get it.''

Randy pulled out the small folder and handed it to the officer. The Latin scanned the papers, then looked back at Stryker, sighing deeply. ''It will be enough, my friend. My superiors will be pleased to assist you in this matter.'' He snapped a command to one of his men. He gestured toward the building that they had been denied access. ''We will wait there while my man summons the good padre.''

''Can a private place be found for us for a few moments?''

''It is only one room. You may use it. We will wait outside.'' The colonel stopped beside the weath-ered door, his eyes slipping over Tempest as she lay against Stryker. ''She has a good man.'' He opened the door himself, closing it after Stryker.

Stryker moved into the dim interior, taking one of three chairs and cradling Tempest across his thighs. He uncapped his canteen and tipped a little against her lips. Her lashes fluttered as she sipped slowly. ''Easy, honey.''

Tempest opened her eyes, sighing as the compara-tive coolness and lack of glare penetrated the fire that seemed to wrap around her to sap her strength. ''I've got a fever again,'' she muttered fretfully.

''Don't talk. Just sip this and listen. We don't have much time.''

Rational thinking was nearly impossible but Stryk-er's tone demanded that she try. ''What's wrong?''

''You don't have your passport.''

"Told you."

"They won't let us leave without it."

Tempest frowned, groping for a solution. "But we have to," she replied finally.

"I know, sweetheart." He brushed the sweat-dampened hair back off her face. "And we're going to leave just like we planned."

She smiled faintly. "You solved the problem." Her eyes started to close. "You always do."

"Don't go to sleep." He shook her gently. "This is important. I need your help."

Tempest forced her eyes open, focusing on his concerned face and wishing vaguely that he wouldn't look so worried. She wanted him smiling, not anxious about her. He had rescued her. It was time to be happy again. "I'll do it."

Stryker felt like yelling in frustration. "You don't know what it is."

"Doesn't matter." The words might have been slurred but the total faith she had in him was clearly audible.

Stryker couldn't remember when he had ever felt so wrong when trying to do something right. "Honey, we have to get married."

That managed to make a dent in the fever cloud. "No, we don't. Not pregnant."

He groaned. "We have to get married so you will have some kind of locally accepted ID to leave the country."

She searched his face, pushing her mind into some kind of working order. Stryker wouldn't lie to her. That fact was clear. And he was too bone deep honest to manipulate her. So far, so good. "Marry, we can go. No marriage and we stay?"

"Yes."

"You could leave me."

"You know better. If you can't do it, we both stay, and if I know Randy, he'll hang in with us as well."

Tempest lifted her arm, feeling as though she were lifting a hundred pounds. She touched his cool cheek. "All right. If that's the only way. Okay."

He pressed her hot, trembling fingers against his skin. He had wanted marriage but not like this. He pulled her palm across his lips, placing a kiss in the center. "Thank you."

Her lashes drifted shut. "No. Thank you for caring for me." She snuggled against him. "Wake me up when I have to say I do."

EIGHT

Tempest tossed fitfully on the narrow couch, feeling tied to the uncomfortable bed. She fought the bonds, groaning as her bruised body thrashed, blindly seeking an escape.

"Easy, girl. Lie still. Stryker's coming back." Randy frowned as she continued to pull at his hold, moaning, using energy she didn't have. He glanced over his shoulder, wishing Stryker would hurry. Every time he had to leave her, Tempest started fretting. No one would do but Stryker.

Tempest felt the chains holding her prisoner tighten, strengthen. "No," she gasped, arching up and trying to break free.

"Stryker!" Randy bellowed as she managed to slip out of his hold.

Tempest heard the shout of a voice she didn't recognize. Her fever made the rough sound merge with the past and the rebels who had attacked the camp.

Terror, an instinct for survival, made her gather her pitiful strength. She had to stay free so that Stryker could find her. Her lashes opened, frantically searching for an escape route.

Randy's bellow woke the rest of the team sleeping in the forward seats. The two men rose, filling Tempest's vision, enlarging on her hallucination. She screamed Stryker's name just as the bathroom door at the rear of the plane burst open and Stryker came out in a rush. He took in the scene in one glance.

"Get back!" he commanded, moving swiftly to Tempest as she sat crouched, trembling and terrified on the couch. His body came between her and the images of the three men seemingly looming over her.

She grabbed at him, tears filling her eyes, her breath whistling out of a congested chest. "I couldn't find you," she whimpered.

Stryker gathered her close, lifting her carefully so as not to disorient her any more. "I had to go to the bathroom," he murmured, settling her into his arms, her head against his heart. The heat of her body was almost unbearable in spite of the air-conditioning of the plane. "You scared Randy to death, honey, screaming like that." He stroked her length gently, easing the tension from her with every sweep of his hand. "I told you I wouldn't leave you. I promised." His croon was pitched low, hopefully soft enough to lull her back into the half sleep that seemed to be the only rest she could handle.

"I'll get you some fresh water and something for her to drink," Randy said quietly, backing away as silently as possible.

Tempest snuggled closer to Stryker. He was so

cool, solid enough to hold at bay the nightmares that waited for her every time she closed her eyes to sleep. "Married yet?" she murmured, drowsing against him.

"Yes." He brushed her heated skin with his lips. When Randy placed a fresh bowl of water and a glass filled with water and tiny ice chips on the table next to him, Stryker eased Tempest into a half-reclining position. "Thirsty?"

"Yes." She drank greedily from the glass he held to her lips, muttering when he only allowed her a few sips at a time. Her mutters became sighs of pleasure when he began sponging her face with the cool water. Relaxing, she let him hold her, keeping the nightmares away and taming the fire that was trying to burn her alive.

"We'll be home soon," Stryker said softly, watching her face, looking for any sign that the fever was easing. "Your family is waiting for us. And Josh has found you a doctor who's a real whiz with tropical fevers. You'll be well soon." He kissed her tenderly, his lips lingering on the elegant curve of her cheek.

"Married is nice," she murmured, before finally giving in to sleep.

Stryker held her, his hand never faltering in the long cooling strokes that were the only relief he could give her. The plane raced toward the east, carrying them home, mission accomplished and complicated by a marriage that he had wanted more with every breath he drew and one that Tempest saw as a trap for one or both of them. He didn't know the future. He wished he did. He didn't know how bad the fever was that was slowly, effectively sapping Tempest's energy. He didn't know how to make her realize that he wanted her, intended to have her no matter how hard she fought him.

He had thought understanding her would mean that he could tame the wildness that drove her to take risks with her life. As he held her loosely but securely in his arms, he knew that he had finally learned the real truth. There was no taming her spirit, no gentling that would make her ever accept the bonds in which others found comfort. Even half out of her mind with fever, she fought any attempt by any hands but his to hold her down. Pain lay in his eyes as he looked on her face, the quiet of her features that was never there when her eyes were open. To keep her, he would have to open his hands and let her fly. That had been their big mistake, his and her family's. All along, each of them, in his own way, had tried to tether the eagle to a stake on the ground. But no more.

It would be a strange marriage he would give her. His heart would be in his throat with every risk she took. He would send her off with his love and worry until she flew back to him. But he would not chain her to his side. She loved him. There would be no other man in her life. She had shown him that without him even asking. She would give what she could. And he would accept because it was the only way to have her. If she was hurt, he would heal her. If she was sick, he would hold her. If she was in trouble, he would rescue her. He smiled faintly, thinking of his future. His job took him all over the world. Her whim chased rainbows and myths without regard to country boundaries. A strange marriage. But each reunion would make it new, bright, forever young. They would play. Tempest was an expert and he would learn. They would dream. And they would fly, together, separately, freely. He would own the wind and be owned by it.

"We'll be landing in fifteen minutes. One of the men will clear this up," Randy whispered. "I'm going up to the cockpit. Need anything?"

"No."

Randy touched his shoulder. "Sorry I let her get so upset."

"It wasn't your fault."

Randy grimaced but said nothing more as he turned away.

A little over an hour later, Stryker had to acknowledge the clout that Arthur and Josh had between them. The ambulance had been waiting as promised, and Tempest had been cleared by a customs official to be taken to the hospital and the isolation room and team that was waiting to receive her. The only glitch in the proceedings was when Dr. Ortiz tried to make him leave the room.

"I'm staying. She gets upset if she's left alone," Stryker said, holding onto Tempest's hand as he faced the slender, dark-eyed doctor.

"It is not possible."

The nurse came to the other side of the bed and wrapped a tourniquet around Tempest's arm to draw blood for the lab work. The moment Tempest felt the stranger's touch, she shifted toward Stryker, muttering. Stryker stroked her cheek. "It's all right. The doctor needs your blood for some tests."

Tempest blinked, trying to focus on Stryker's face in the bright glare of the all-white room. "Already married. Don't need blood test."

He bent so that she could see him better. "Definitely married." He kissed the hand that he held and started to tuck it under the blanket at her side. "I have to get out of the way so they can examine you, but I'm not leaving."

She grabbed his fingers, struggling to understand, but only one fact made any impression. He was leaving. "No! You promised."

Dr. Ortiz moved closer. "It won't take long, Mrs. McGuire. We will be quick."

Frantic, feeling abandoned, not knowing the face with the dark eyes that so reminded her of the rebels who had attacked the camp, Tempest responded only on instinct. "No! Leave me alone. Don't know you." She tried to get up. The nurse caught her before Stryker could reach around the doctor. With her head turned toward the men, Tempest was shocked by the hands trying to restrain her. She fought, gasping for breath with the effort. Stryker swore, pushing the doctor out of the way.

"Leave her alone, damn it." He yanked the nurse's hands away and caught Tempest to him. "Stop it, honey. Quiet down. It's all right." Her face was pressed against his neck, her breath hot. Her hands clenched his shirt as though she would never let him go.

"Make them go away. Go away. Just hold me."

The doctor sighed and signaled the nurse to back away for a moment. "I see what you mean. You hold her and we will do the best we can. First the blood."

Stryker unlatched one hand, extended the limb, bracing her with his strength. "Don't move. Not an inch."

Tempest nodded against his heart. "Okay."

The blood was drawn with no problem. Then the exam, tricky but accomplished with the same docility from Tempest as she showed for the blood test. Finally the preliminary check was complete.

"I think I know this fever and I will go on that knowledge until the tests can confirm my thinking. She is very ill. I cannot pretend otherwise, but if I am right, this fever shouldn't get much worse than it is now. Only the very young or the very old and weak die from it. She is strong, healthy, and a fighter." He smiled faintly as he nodded toward their linked hands and the way that Tempest, even half asleep, seemed to curve toward Stryker as he sat on the edge of her bed. "And she has much to live for."

"Why didn't the antibiotic I pumped into her work?"

"Not strong enough or specific enough. We shall do better, you will see. But she will be very confused, much as she is right now. Friends may be enemies and she will look for only the one she trusts. You. And you are tired yourself."

"I'll survive. Knowing it isn't as bad as I was beginning to think is enough."

The doctor inclined his head. "I will bend the rules for you and her. There will be an extra bed in her room. Use it if you can. If I am right, she will be like this for as many as three days before we can start winning the battle.''

"You look like hell,'' Arthur observed, looking Stryker over carefully as he took the chair beside Tempest's bed. "Let one of us stay with her for a while so you can rest, really rest.''

Stryker massaged the back of his neck with his free hand. Less than an hour before he had been holding Tempest as she had relived the bombing of the shed and the twenty-four hours she had spent hiding while the rebels ransacked the relief camp. She had cried, something he was positive she hadn't done at the time. Those tears still lingered in his memory.

"I don't think it would work,'' he said finally, wearily. "For whatever reason, I can't go farther than the bathroom without her waking up. And the doctor says she needs all the sleep she can get.''

Arthur frowned, having heard firsthand the strange connection that existed between his daughter and the man he had always sent to her aid. "It seems that I am always asking you to help her. Maybe too much. I hadn't realized she'd hang on like this. I wouldn't have even thought it was in her makeup to latch on to anyone for any reason.'' He studied his daughter, trying to find some frame of reference, some characteristic that he shared with this, the youngest of his offspring. But there was none. No trait, no common interest, no real understanding. He regretted the distance between them but he was helpless to bridge it. "I don't know how to thank you for marrying her just to get her out of that country. My lawyers say there won't be any problem with an annulment as soon as she's strong enough to sign the papers."

Tempest heard the voices speaking in low tones, recognizing both as men she loved. One hopelessly, one helplessly.

"There will be no annulment."

Arthur's brows rose at the flat statement. "Meaning?"

"That's between me and Tempest, but there will be no annulment."

"Are you saying that you and she are lovers?"

"I'm saying nothing, admitting or denying nothing. I wanted to marry Tempest before that damn colonel started to flex his muscles. She didn't want to marry me."

"Why?"

"Why which?"

"Why did you want to marry her? I know you well enough not to think you're a fortune hunter. You know what she's like. You won't have a home life, a family, or anything that any man would expect to have with a woman. Hell, she's never in one place long enough even to have a relationship."

Stryker stared at the man he had always admired and suddenly found another piece to fit into the picture that was beginning to emerge of Tempest. "Maybe I don't want those things."

Tempest struggled to lift her lashes. Her father was pushing Stryker, forcing him to defend her. She hated the words that were bouncing across the bed. She could hear the controlled anger in Stryker's voice. She squeezed his hand, gathering her strength to speak.

"Do you?" she whispered, finally able to focus on his face.

Stryker touched her cheek, relieved to feel the heat slowly leaching away for longer periods. Finally, he understood her. "No chains, my eagle. You can fly anytime you want."

"Come with me?" She searched his face, wishing her thinking weren't so muddled, wishing she could lift her head without feeling as though she were lifting the world on her neck.

"When I can." He brushed her lips. "Now stop talking to me and say hello to your father. He's been waiting two days for you to notice he's here."

Tempest ignored the coaxing words for the more important issue, her dream that she never thought to have. "Promise?"

He smiled, his dark eyes lighting with humor and acceptance. "I promise. No chains. I'll hold you only when you ask me to."

"You love me."

"Yes. No conditions. No strings and no in spite ofs."

Her smile was beautiful, real and very Tempest. Joy shone in blue eyes that had held only listless acceptance of the passage of the last few days. "I'll be careful."

Stryker glanced down, not wanting her to see that this one promise he knew better than to believe. She meant it. She would even try. But she wouldn't succeed. And one day, a capricious hand of nature or fate might just snuff the light from her eyes and rip the heart out of his body before he could get to her for one last rescue.

"Then we're both happy," he murmured, lifting her hand to his lips. When he knew she wouldn't be able to read anything but love in his eyes, he looked back at her. "Now, speak to your father before he decides to fire me, wife."

Tempest turned her head, looking at her father. "Iii."

Arthur started to open his mouth to deliver the lecture that had been seething in his mind. Then he really studied her wan features and the trembling but determined grip she had on Stryker's hand. He couldn't remember when he had seen her so weak. He swallowed his words unsaid. "Hi, yourself." He leaned down and kissed her cheek. "Feel like saying hello to your mother and your brother and sister. They're waiting in the hall."

"Okay."

He rose, glancing at Stryker, seeing approval for his restraint and understanding for the words he had wanted to say. He wondered how he had missed the affinity his daughter and this man he admired shared. He was not usually so blind.

Tempest stared out the window of her hospital room. Dawn was unfurling its rose and gold banner of color, veiling the lingering shadows of the night with vibrant shades that invited those still sleeping to awake and bask in the glory of a new day. She cupped her hands under her chin, leaning her head against the cool glass, wishing the window could be opened so that she could inhale the day. She was alone, had been alone for the past three nights. She would leave this place today. The fever was gone.

Seven days of fire and hell were over. She had lost weight and strength. Just getting up seemed to tire her right now. But at least she could sleep without nightmares. At least she had stopped hanging on to Stryker as if he was the only lifeline she had in a sea of people she didn't know and didn't trust. Even now she couldn't believe what she had done. Her whole family had hinted at her behavior being decidedly odd. The nurses thought it romantic, teasing her gently. And the doctor. Only Stryker had seen her embarrassment and explained what had happened. She thought again of his tenderness when she had blurted out an awkward apology.

"Stop worrying about it, honey," he had murmured, kissing her hand, the hand that had grabbed for him the moment he had come close enough for her to touch. "The doctor and nurse who have been in here the most look very like the rebels. Both have noticeable accents and you were half out of your mind with fever. I was the only one you knew. If the positions had been reversed, I'd have done the same thing."

She remembered laughing at that. His kiss had stopped the laughter, bringing warmth that had nothing to do with fever. She had clung to him then, not her lifeline this time, but the man who had taught her passion and love.

Stryker stood in the open doorway of Tempest's room, watching her stare out the window. Yearning was in every curve of her body. His hands clenched at his side. Already it was starting. Already he was fighting the need to tie her to him. He inhaled deeply, slowly, pushing back the need to hold her and remembering all the reasons that he could not.

"Ready to be sprung from this place?" he asked lazily, feeling anything but.

Tempest twisted around in the chair, a smile lighting her eyes and curving her lips. She jumped to her feet, took three quick steps toward him before dizziness at the sudden movements caught up with her. Before she could fall or do more than sway, she was in his arms, pressed against his chest. "I hate being this weak," she muttered, rubbing her forehead against his heart as she hugged him.

Stryker kissed the crown of bright hair, grinning a little at the unconcealed disgust in her voice. "Well, if you wouldn't continue to act as if you're superhuman with no recovery period needed, you wouldn't be so quick to show off you are still weak."

She lifted her head, trying to glare at him. But it was so good to have him hold her, to know that soon they would be away from this place, that she laughed instead. "I hate it when you're right."

He kissed her nose, then swung her up in his arms to carry her to the bed.

"This is getting to be a habit."

"I like it. Don't you?"

"I shouldn't." She touched his cheek as he settled her amid the rumpled covers and then sat down next to her hip. The waiting look in his eyes made her finish the sentence. "But, yes, I do like it."

"Good."

Her brows arched. "Is that all you're going to say?"

"Yes."

"Rat."

"Husband," he corrected.

Her amusement died. She glanced down at his hands as they held his weight braced on either side of her body.

"What is it?"

"What are we going to do about being married?"

He lifted her chin so that he could see her eyes. The worried expression tore at his soul, but he didn't let her see. "I thought we had decided that it would stand. What did you think I was doing, humoring you or playing to your father?"

She studied his face, looking for some hint of what he was thinking or feeling and finding nothing but her own reflection in his eyes. "It's possible," she murmured quietly.

"Possible but not likely. Not for me and you should know that."

"I don't know how to be a wife."

"So what? I've got no practice at being a husband."

"My father was right. You won't have the things you should be able to expect with me. I *can't* live with routine." Feeling panicked at the thought of the demands that surely must be waiting in her future, she twisted her hands in the sheets.

"Stop that." Stryker loosened her fingers, threading his own through them. "I'm not stupid. I'll admit I haven't been very smart where you're concerned in the past. I thought you were playing at getting yourself killed in the most spectacular way possible and that made me angry. I finally see that I was wrong. I wish you had felt safe enough with me to explain, but considering the fact that every time you turned around I was shouting at you about one of your stunts, I can understand why you didn't.''

"You're making it sound like your fault."

He shook his head. "No. It's no one's fault. I believe every one of us is born with certain needs. Environment plays a part but a lot of what we do is there from the moment of birth. You can't help needing to climb mountains because they're there. If you were a man, the world would see your actions in a different light. Your family would accept them, probably even take pride in your exploits.''

Tears filled her eyes, dancing on her lashes. He brushed away the few that fell off the tips with a gentle forefinger. "I don't want you to conform. You'd hate that and eventually me. I married you, knowing exactly what you are. Who better? Even your family doesn't know the full extent of things you've done. No, we won't have an ordinary relationship. Nine-to-five jobs. Two point five kiddies and roses in the garden. I'm not even sure I could live that scenario myself. I travel. You're not asking me to give that up.''

"I can go with you," she offered eagerly, beginning to accept he understood.

"As much as you like."

"Always."

He cupped her cheek, stroking the pale skin that was now cool to his touch. "Don't make promises you can't keep. That's one of the only two rules in this marriage we're creating. You might want to go with me every time, but one day, there will be something on the horizon that will matter more. You'll hate leaving, but the pull will be so strong that you'll obey it and go. I accept that. You must as well.''

Tempest looked into his eyes, hearing truths that no one had ever spoken before. She had prayed so often for someone to understand the demons that drove her to search the world for the new, the exciting, the unique. But now that she was facing his knowledge of her, she was beginning to feel uncomfortable with the image. Appalled, when she had spent years defending her right to complete freedom, she turned her face into the palm of his hand.

''I sound terrible.''

He stroked the flame-colored hair that swirled about her shoulders, aching for her, knowing that her life would cost him countless hours of worry but that she paid a higher price for her freedom than he. ''No, just my Tempest.''

''How can you love me?''

He laughed softly, deeply at that. ''I didn't want to, believe me. You're a hellion and I'm a man who hates unsolvable problems. But I can't help myself. Neither one of us can tame our demons, it would seem.''

She lifted her head, stunned at his amusement and his reply. ''I'm your demon.''

He pulled her against him, tipping her head over his arm, exposing the slender line of her throat, the pulse beating there, marking every breath of her life. ''Definitely that and so much more that I can't begin to tell you what you mean to me.''

Thrusting her hands into the dark pelt of his hair, she brought his head down. Her lips brushed his, tasting, needing, wanting in ways she hadn't allowed free rein since that first moment of passion, that moment when she had willingly given up her innocence. "I will love you until I die. No matter how far I fly or how high, know that if you don't know anything else. For as long as you want me I will always return." She covered his mouth with hers, wanting not his words, only his love.

He met her more than halfway, taking her gift, sharing the emotional flight that only Tempest could give him. He stroked her length, molding her to him, hating the gown and his clothes. Her taste was sweeter than he remembered, fuller, more demanding and yet equally more giving. He inhaled her fragrance, knowing it would haunt him through the many lonely nights that were his future, knowing too that to deny her those nights was a living death for them both. When he raised his head, her lips were red from his possession, her eyes dark with passion unfulfilled. He traced the full outline, then smoothed the fine flesh of her throat, his fingers lingering on the pulse in the hollow. "How soon can you get dressed?"

"I want to say seconds but minutes will do." She searched his eyes, finding no shadows there, only loving.

"Then hurry. We have a plane to catch."

NINE

The Bahamas lay like a string of white freshwater pearls, dotted with green on a bed of turquoise and blue satin. The sun shone on the islands, the temperature, at this time of year, mild enough to be pleasant without the draining heat of midsummer. Tempest peered out the window of the Luck Enterprises corporate jet as they landed in Nassau.

"I didn't really think you were serious about coming down here," she said, turning to face Stryker. "How did you get the doctor to agree?"

She looked better, he decided, studying the healthy color of her skin, the bright, inquisitive look in her eyes. "Didn't you wonder why you had to stay in the hospital so long after you were clearly on the mend?"

"I thought it had something to do with the fever recurring."

He shook his head, grinning. "No. It had to do

with me wanting my honeymoon and being determined to have it. You, my wife, were the victim of a conspiracy. The doctor kept you in until he was sure you were strong enough for the flight. My orders are to see that you get plenty of rest and do nothing more exciting than lazing around.''

''Really!'' Her brows rose, her eyes glinting with challenge.

He kissed her nose, laughing when she wrinkled it at him. ''Yes, really, babe. You and I are headed for a tiny little island that has no way off but the seaplane that is going to take us there. There's a house and a pool and a beach with enough white sand to tempt a water baby like you into coming out to play.''

''And what will you be doing all this time?'' She cupped her chin in her hands, propped her elbows on the arms of the seat, and watched him.

''I'll be seeing that you spend a lot of time in bed. Getting your rest, you know.''

She laughed, the sound rippling around them like chimes of tiny silver bells stirred by a capricious breeze. ''You will, will you? Don't I have anything to say about this program?''

''Not a thing. This is my honeymoon. You are just along so that you can get strong enough to fly.'' He kissed her quickly, thoroughly, but teasingly. He missed the strange flash of pain in her eyes. He caught her hand, directing her eyes toward the window. ''Look out there. Those are the last signs of people you'll be seeing for a whole two weeks.''

''I won't mind,'' she said softly, leaning her head against his shoulder.

"Tired?" His voice was a whiskey-rich rumble in her ear.

"A little. I'll be glad when I'm completely well."

"Fevers take a lot out of you. I've had a couple in my time."

She frowned slightly at the thought of him hurting and lost in the maze of fire and pain that she had just come through. He had been there to hold her hand, to be the center of her mad, confusing world. But who had been there for him? She turned her face, catching his lips, kissing him with sudden urgency. When she released him, she read the question in his eyes. "I never realized. After all those times you've rescued me, I've never done the same for you. Did you ever need someone? Or are you really as self-sufficient as you seem?"

Her comments surprised him but he had promised her the truth. "I don't know how I seem. I do know that I get lonely." His arm curled around her waist. Neither noticed the plane touching down. "I miss you, often. Most of the time, I told myself that I didn't really want to see you because that meant trouble and probably danger of some kind for you."

"I don't know how you can love me."

"I didn't want to."

Her quick laugh held no amusement. "I'm not sure your brand of honesty is something I want."

He turned her to face him, searching her eyes. "Isn't it? A lie, no matter how well meant, hurts in the end."

"True. But the truth can hurt as well."

"It is also freedom. Your battle cry."

"Perhaps." She hated the pain of knowing that he had fought loving her.

He saw the flash of hurt in her gaze, understood it, and softened the truth with more of the same. "But I couldn't stop what I was feeling. Not with anyone or anything. It was . . . is that strong."

She stared at him, looking for a sop to her wounded heart and finding only fact without blemish. "I've wanted to belong to you since I was fifteen years old. You walked into the head's office and listened without a blink to that tale of lies he told you. I waited and waited for you to berate me, point out my stupidity, tell me how I was wasting myself. It never happened. You just asked me what was really going on."

He, too, remembered that first time. The anger in the too old eyes set in the too controlled young face. She had stood before her accuser listening without any visible sign of distress to a complete assassination of her character and morals. He should have believed the headmaster. Her family certainly had. But something about her had whispered of condemnation expected and accepted but falsely laid at her door.

"You told me nothing," he murmured.

"I cursed you," she corrected. "Did I ever say I was sorry for all those horrible names?"

"No."

She kissed his cheek. "I am. That is from me then."

He looked at her mouth, wanting more than a gentle gesture from a child who hadn't been gentle even then. "I'd prefer a kiss from my wife."

"Can't." She nodded toward the terminal that was coming closer with every second. "Not here. Or now."

"The island?"

"Yes."

The island that would be their home for two weeks lay drowsing in the sun, an emerald and pearl piece of nature's handiwork surrounded by a calm sea just waiting to be explored. From the air, only a tiny square of bright red tile roof too perfect in line to be drawn by other than man was the only indication that this Eden, unlike its neighbors, was inhabited. The seaplane skimmed the water, throwing out froths of white to streak a path to the small dock that lay like a pointing finger in the tiny bay on the south side. It took only a few moments for Tempest and Stryker to disembark, then the plane was easing away, their last touch of communication with the outside world for fourteen days.

"What do you think?" Stryker asked without even looking around the island. He had stayed there once before when he had set up a deal with one of the local businesses in Nassau.

"How can I tell from here?" she replied teasingly as she bent to pick up her case.

Stryker took it from her, ignoring her quick frown. "You can be the packhorse when we leave."

"I hate it when you're reasonable. Why can't you go back to ordering me around?"

He chuckled as he followed her up the dock. "It never worked all that well. Even if I could force you into taking care of yourself or learning something to help you in the future, I always felt guilty as hell afterwards.''

She stopped, swinging around quickly to study him. ''Really?''

He nodded, his eyes serious in spite of the slight smile on his face. ''Really. Why do you think I went through that survival course with you when I had already done the thing once? I hated it just as much the second time around.''

She propped her hands on her hips, recalling that nightmare. ''You rat. You spent the whole ten days telling me that you enjoyed that sadistic course. My muscles hurt every time I think of it and now you tell me that you hated it, too. I ate creepy crawlies I've never heard of then or since. Even in the damn jungle I didn't have to resort to that.'' Her eyes flashed as she tossed her head in the beginnings of a very real temper. Sun caught at the red strands, setting them alight.

Stryker tipped back his head, laughing. He dropped the cases just as she launched herself at him. He caught her easily, swinging her up, off the ground, holding her aloft as she glared at him. ''I did enjoy the course. I enjoyed knowing that no matter what, you could take it. It was the most secure I had ever felt to that point. Up until then I had accepted and believed as your family did. That because you look as fragile as a small doll and haven't ever really known hardship and had a tendency to act before you considered the consequences that you were a bit of fluff playing at being a rebel.''

Tempest grabbed his shoulders, more to steady her mental processes than her physical position. Every bit of temper died. "That was the year you gave me the knife." Releasing him with one hand, she dug into the pocket of her dress and brought out the Swiss knife that had more gadgets than she had needed so far. "I never forgot." She held it up between them, looking at it, remembering the times it had saved her skin, remembering the times she had simply held it in her hands to remind her that someone cared about her enough to see her equipped for the life she wanted to lead even when that life didn't meet with his approval. "Sometimes, when I was all alone, missing home, tired, discouraged, or hungry, I would hold this and think of you." She lifted her head, looking at him as though he were her world. In so many ways he was, she realized. He had colored her existence for so many years, taking her side in ways that she was just now beginning to understand.

Stryker lowered her to the sand, easing her body down his length so that both of them were aware of every curve and angle of the other. His eyes glittered with the need that was slowly uncurling within him. He watched her lips part, her fingers tighten on his gift. "I found it in the jungle when I undressed you," he murmured deeply, pressing his hands to her lower body, angling her hips so that they rested completely in the cradle of his thighs.

"We should get up to the house."

He looked past her to the short, sandy trail beneath the trees. Lifting her, he kissed her deeply, letting her know that the delay would be as short as he could make it. "We'll get the luggage later."

Tempest wrapped her arms around his neck, no longer objecting to his habit of carrying her at the least opportunity. "Much later," she agreed with a husky catch in her voice. She nipped at his ear, hardly noticing the wild gardens that protected the privacy of the house from the open view of the sea. The cool of the interior after the heat of the sun was a balm, and the room into which he carried her was dim and quiet. The shutters on the windows allowed vistas of the gardens and the ocean but screened them in a world holding only them and the passion that tied them together.

Stryker set her on her feet beside the bed, his hands sliding over her shoulders until he found the narrow ties that held the teal green sundress she was wearing. He released the bows, then brushed a kiss over each bare shoulder. Tempest stood still, letting him lead as she never had before. It wasn't that she was shy, rather that just this once she wanted to be a woman who submitted completely to her man. She wanted to give Stryker every part of her, to know that every inch of her skin, her heart, her thoughts was his. She wanted him to find completion in her arms, a union so profound that no matter what she did he would remember this moment and the love she offered.

"So quiet," Stryker whispered against her throat, his tongue tracing the throb of her pulse in the vulnerable hollow. He outlined the top of the bodice, the tips of his fingers edging under the fabric, easing it downward by slow inches. Her breathing broke in husky little gasps, her hands curled into the front of his shirt, holding on as though to let go was to lose her balance.

"I love you."

The words, whispered with such depth of emotion, slipped into his soul, filling the emptiness shading the past, the present, and the future that would carry shadows of her needs that would never include him. He raised his head for a moment, facing her and the imperfect future that was his cross for loving her. "We love each other."

Her hands dipped into his hair, pulling his mouth close. "Forever and forever."

Her kiss was sweet, tender as it had never been. Tears were in her eyes as he pulled the dress from her body, leaving her in a tiny pair of green panties and white sandals. He skimmed her curves, lingering over her breasts, teasing her nipples until they bloomed as perfectly as hothouse roses. She arched toward him, silently begging for his touch but making no move to hurry him beyond that. She wanted every second to last a year, every breath to be a day. She could feel the fire, the fever, but this one fed rather than depleted her. Her hips rotated, brushing him, teasing him as his mouth tugged at her nipple, suckling with masculine hunger that tightened her muscles and whipped her nerve endings so they tingled with sensation. She sucked in her breath as his hands slipped lower, rimming the top of her panties, dipping beneath, then retreating without satisfying. Her hips bucked with each thrust, demanding more in spite of her wish to prolong every second of this joining.

"Don't tease. I want you too much," she groaned against his mouth just before he stole her breath and any more protests. His taste filled her, driving out rational thought, tapping the instincts that had lain dormant within her since he had shared that first initiation. The first time she had offered herself knowing there was no future but hoping anyway. This time, she gave herself, knowing the future and not needing hope, for Stryker had not demanded anything of her that she could not give.

Passion took flight with every stroke. The wings of her desire lifted on the thermals of hot need. Her legs felt too weak to hold her as his mouth drifted down her body, his hands baring her femininity to his look, his touch. Her nails dug into his shoulders as she curved over him, her breasts seeking the strength of his back, the warmth that chased the cool of the room away. He caressed her legs, long sweeps to measure her limbs from thigh to ankle as he traced the boundaries of the curls that guarded the secrets of her strength and weakness to him.

"Stryker." His name was a plea spoken in a voice made soft as a breath by his hand.

Stryker rose from his knees, taking her weight and carrying her to the bed. He came down beside her, never pausing in the pleasure he drew from her, and gave to himself in each gasp of delight, each moan of surrender. He watched the passion blush tint her skin. He etched each change of her body in his memory. When she fumbled at the buttons of his shirt, he helped her, finally taking over to strip as swiftly as possible so that the separation was over almost before it had begun. He entered her, looking into her eyes, watching the tears drench the sky blue, hearing his name cried out in the silence, broken, shattered sounds that echoed the crumbling of any defenses he had against this woman now and in the future. Then he gathered her to him, thrusting for the peak that would burn them both alive.

He called her name. She answered with a wild demand that commanded the full range of his passion to join with her. There was no gentleness in the way they fought to reach the center of the storm. His body and hers would carry bruises for days to come. It didn't matter. He was strong. And so was she. The end and the beginning came as a volcano at the instant of the creation of new life.

Fire sizzling, moisture too little to cage the flames, bodies fighting the pain of rebirth, embracing the release with sighs so deep that their flesh rippled with the effort. Then whispers, words with meaning beyond definition. Then sleep, a healing offered by the very gods who had decreed that man and woman must always come together fighting pain and pleasure to find heaven in each other's arms.

"I can't believe you're too shy to take off your suit and swim with me nude." Stryker stared at his wife as she lay on her stomach pretending to sleep on the blanket next to him. They had spent the last three days more in bed than out. There wasn't an inch of her skin that he didn't know intimately. They had showered together, played together in the shelter of the house as she had followed the doctor's orders. This was the first day they had ventured to the beach for more than an early morning or late evening walk.

"It isn't a question of swimming with you nude. It's a matter of swimming in the open nude," she muttered, keeping her face turned into her arms. She hadn't known she was shy until Stryker's suggestion.

Stryker frowned, not positive she wasn't teasing. "There's no one around."

"I know." She sighed, rolled over, and looked up at him. "It's dumb. I admit it. But I don't think I can do it."

Touched by the defiant admission, he stroked her sun-warmed cheek with a gentle finger. "All right. Suppose we get into the water in our suits and then strip."

She shivered with the soft caress, no longer amazed at the tenderness that almost always lived in his touch for her. "You're determined about this, aren't you?"

"Well, I've been thinking about it for three days. Male fantasy or something." He shrugged, bending his head to kiss her shoulder. Then he nipped at her ear, feeling the expected quivers of reaction race over her skin.

"Dirty pool," she murmured, turning into his caress as her hands stroked his chest, tangling in the dark hair to tug gently.

"Coward."

She kissed the tight male nipple that seemed to be demanding her attention. "That's sneaky."

He plucked lightly at her breast through the fabric of her bikini, rubbing the tiny nub until she arched to him. "Did it work?"

Her voice was husky with the need he was creating. "You know I can't resist a challenge."

He gathered her close and brushed the hair back from her face as he looked deeply into her eyes. "It's what I'm counting on."

She sighed and looped her arms around his shoulders, no longer hesitant about his suggestion. Suddenly, she wanted to be bare in this primitive setting. "It will cost you a ride to the water."

"You changed your mind," Stryker murmured huskily, reading her decision in the flash of curiosity and passion in her eyes. He laughed softly, not triumphantly but gladly as he sat up and pulled her into his lap. He skimmed the suit off her slender body, his hands lingering over each curve, enjoying the return of her former sleek figure that the time here had given her.

Tempest felt the kiss of the sun everywhere. She stretched sinuously in his arms, smiling at the hunger that glittered brightly in his eyes. "You wanted to swim," she whispered.

"I've changed my mind."

"Can't."

He caught her left nipple before she could realize that he hadn't been lowering his head to kiss her lips. Tempest moaned softly as he teased her with erotic pulls on the taut peak. She arched closer as the rhythm increased. "Still want to go swimming?" he demanded, raising his head.

"Yes, damn you," she replied, sliding her fingers into the front of his briefs to tease him in return. His sharp inhalation pleased her almost as much as his caresses. "You're getting too arrogant, my lover. Much too arrogant."

Tumbling her onto the blanket, he rose on his knees and yanked off his suit. Before she could right herself, Stryker had come to his feet with her in his arms.

"I should have known better than to play with fire with a woman named Tempest."

She bit his shoulder, leaving marks but not breaking the skin. "So you should," she agreed huskily as he lowered her into the warm sea.

The law office of Beattle, Todd and Marchant was solidly conservative, as befitted one of the first partnerships in Richmond's legal community. Southern traditions still lived and flourished in Virginia and none were more strictly adhered to than those performed by this office for its elite and influential clients. There were a number of flashier firms in town, certainly some as large, but none had the cachet of B. T. and M. To be one of its patrons, one must have old money, strong family ties, and interests in any number of arenas. In short, B. T. and M. didn't handle the ordinary, only the uniquely extraordinary. Which was why old Miss Tempest Whitney was one of its more well-known clients, certainly the most eccentric, before or after her marriage to Rufus King. What other woman of her era, especially one who was known for her genteel manners and self-effacing personality, would prove so stubborn about taking up her maiden name on the day she was made a widow by a freak flash flood that had taken the brand new Buick and her not so new husband away? When she had died four years ago, her will had caused just as much whispering in the country club and around the tea table as her married life and subsequent widowhood had done.

Now old Mr. Marchant, contemporary of Tempest Whitney, sat at his carved antique desk, frowning at the announcement in front of him. Tempest Whitney-King had finally gotten married, an event her family had almost given up praying for. But that wasn't what had dug the lines of concern into his aged face. The man she had married was just the man whose name had plagued him for the past four years and three months, since the moment the older Tempest had summoned him in the middle of the night, something no one but she would have gotten away with, and changed her will. He glanced at the will that lay beside the announcement. Even if he had not prepared the thing himself, he would have known the words by heart.

He picked up the phone and dialed Arthur King. Ten minutes later, his frown was deeper, and one mutter that was as close to a curse as he had ever allowed himself had passed his lips. He couldn't reach the newlyweds until they returned from their island honeymoon. Exactly two days from now. He buzzed his secretary, giving her the orders he had been dreading since Miss Tempest had died and left him with this unholy situation.

"Please, book me a seat on a flight to Houston three days from today. And a hotel room that isn't near the airport."

TEN

Tempest leaned against her husband's side, staring out the window of the limo her father had sent to meet them at the airport. She wasn't looking forward to this interview with her family. Because she had been so ill, not one of her relatives had taken her to task for the debacle of Central America and certainly none of them had confronted her about her subsequent marriage to Stryker. She knew better than to expect that state of affairs to hold this time and definitely not when the chauffeur, a longtime and well-valued employee of the family, had subtly let her know that the family was gathered and waiting for her and Stryker at the main house.

"Stop looking as if you're going to your own execution," Stryker commanded, slipping his fingers into her clenched fists until her hands relaxed in his. "I'll be there and I promise they won't say much of anything anyway."

She looked at him, cynicism that she rarely allowed to show flashing in her eyes. "I'm used to their lectures on what is due my name and safety. This time I doubt I'll get that. More than likely I'll be congratulated on finally doing something right even if I did go about it in typical Tempest fashion."

He couldn't deny the charge, so he didn't try. Once Arthur and the rest of them had gotten over the shock, the whole family had expressed those sentiments, almost in the same words. He hadn't appreciated them then, nor the subtle sympathy and relief they had shown as well. He knew what their attitude would do to Tempest and he ached for her, knowing there was little he could do to solve this problem. He could only be there, at her side, sharing her moments, holding her. "They love you."

"And I love them." She sighed and started to turn back to the futile survey of the passing scenery.

Stryker caught her chin, bringing her face around to his. Words he had wanted to say for years would no longer be denied. "When will you stop feeling guilty for not being like them?"

Startled, Tempest stared. No one had ever said that to her before. "I'm not feeling gui . . ." Her voice died as she realized that she was indeed feeling just that. Guilty because she wasn't her so perfect brother and sister. She didn't follow the rules but in her heart of hearts she wanted to. "I didn't know," she whispered.

He wrapped an arm around her shoulders and pulled her close. Tears that were more easily shed now were in her eyes. "You've been too busy fighting for your life to know. And too young."

Tempest tucked her head against his heart, wrapped in more emotion than she would have thought even she was capable of knowing. She felt secure in ways that she was just beginning to understand. Stryker knew things about her but he never used them against her. He gave her lights to shine on her shadows and held her hand while she peered into the dark corners of her thoughts. He was her partner in the truest and best sense of the word.

"How did you know?"

"It wasn't hard to figure out as soon as I stopped reacting to you and starting thinking. I'm the problem solver, remember. And you, my loving wife, are the most complicated problem I've ever faced." He tipped her face up and brushed her lips. He smiled as he wiped the tears from her eyes. "You drive me to distraction but you're my distraction. It's my thinking and yours that should matter to you now. Not theirs. I know what you are. I accept who you are and what you have to do. I'm not always going to like what you do. And I'm not always going to suffer in silence. But I will keep loving you But you have to start loving yourself. Stop letting them have the power to drive you over the edge. Every time they come down hard, you do something more outrageous than the thing that has driven them to jump you in the first place."

She stared at him, thinking. He was right. In all the years she had fought the label of rebellion and he was showing her that she was both a free spirit and a rebel. She didn't like the knowledge and from anyone else she would have fought it. From Stryker she accepted and learned.

"I've been blind."

"Young."

She smiled faintly. "Yes, wise old husband."

He tapped her hip lightly, his eyes promising all kinds of pleasurable retribution. "Be quiet, brat. We're here."

Tempest glanced around, realizing that not only had they arrived while she had gained new insights into herself but she had lost the tense, nervy feeling that had been dogging her footsteps since they had landed in Houston.

Stryker stepped out of the car and held out his hand. "Ready to beard the lions and lionesses in their dens?"

Tempest took his hand, letting him pull her to his side. She laughed up at him, her eyes sparkling with mischief that held no taint of restraint. "Definitely. Then we can go home to your apartment. Do you realize that I've never been there?" She tucked her arm in his as they mounted the steps together.

"You may not want to stay after you see it. It looks more like a hotel room than a home."

"Then I'll redecorate or we'll look for somewhere nice we both like."

The door opened before they could ring the bell. The butler forgot himself enough to smile. "The staff and I would like to offer our best wishes."

Tempest grinned, glancing up at Stryker, who extended his hand to the older man. "Thank everyone for us, Benton," she said, looking back to the man who appeared as if he would have had little time for children and who, often, had spent precious minutes out of his busy schedule telling her stories and listening to her young woes.

He inclined his head before gesturing toward the salon. "They are waiting for you. I believe they are expecting you to join them for lunch. Cook has made a cake."

"Chocolate with white chocolate icing?"

His smile widened briefly. "Just so, Mrs. Tempest."

She laughed softly. "I like it, Benton," she said, referring to her new title. "Miss Tempest to Mrs. Tempest."

Stryker urged her toward the salon. "Try to look serious, my love," he suggested.

She giggled just as Benton opened the door to the room holding the gathering of the clan. The picture that greeted the eyes of her relatives was one of complete unconcern, youth, and happiness. Tempest was wearing a brief sundress of white on white. Sandals of the same color showed off long legs beneath the frothy hem that danced two inches above her knees. Her skin was gilded gold by the sun and her hair streaked with the same shades so that it appeared she had brought a piece of the islands home with her. Stryker stood tall at her side, his head angled toward hers, his body seeming to hover protectively without caging her with his strength.

Arthur stepped forward, automatically seeking to take command. "You're late. Was there a problem with the plane or the luggage?"

His brows raised, his glance acknowledging the tactic but not unduly bothered by it, Stryker faced his employer/father-in-law. "No. Everything went smoothly."

"We set lunch back an hour so you will have time to freshen up. Your luggage will already be on the way up now."

Tempest tensed at her father's automatic assumption that they would stay the night. She started to protest but the faint warning pressure of Stryker's hand stilled her words.

"We appreciate the invitation, Arthur, but I think we'll just stay for lunch. I haven't shown Tempest our apartment yet."

Arthur frowned, his eyes snapping to his daughter, then back to the man she had married. He might pay Stryker's salary but he had never owned the man, only leased his considerable skill. "Surely you would be more comfortable here. Tempest isn't used to doing for herself."

Tempest felt the subtle sarcasm bite into her happiness. She fought the urge to defend herself with an attack.

Stryker smiled down at her, ignoring the older man. "Actually, she's a good cook. Certainly inventive." His lips twitched with a memory that his glance shared with his wife before he drew her deeper into the room to the small loveseat rather than two of the number of empty chairs that remained unfilled.

Tempest laughed as she settled beside him and faced her family. It was impossible to care what her family thought when Stryker's every look approved her virtues and gently accepted her flaws. His laughter might come when she did something less than perfectly but it would never be cutting or cruel. He would share her mistakes, loving her. The knowledge was one more facet to add to all the rest, another key to a different lock of the cage that her family's needs had built around her. "What he means is that I mixed up some spices on this recipe a friend gave me. We had a very odd version of spaghetti one night."

"Cooking always takes a lot of painstaking work," Tempest's sister murmured, clearly struggling to find some excuse for Tempest's failure. "Much more my personality than Temp's, father."

"Thanks, Lavendar," Tempest said, for once not resenting her sister's attempt to soften her supposed lack of expertise.

Lavendar blinked at the definite sincerity of her response. She looked closer but before she could make a comment, Roger spoke.

"There's really no reason not to stay. It will give us all a better chance to get to know you, Stryker." Of all of them he had had the least contact with the man brave enough to take on his daring sister.

"Would you want to spend your honeymoon with your in-laws?" Stryker asked, eyeing the younger man.

Roger stared at him, the blunt question throwing him off stride. He wasn't a quick thinker, but rather a methodical one. His strength was his ability to take a stand and make it work against all odds. "But you two got married to help Tempest."

"So?"

A flush crawled up his cheeks as he glanced to his father for help. Arthur turned his back and returned to his place beside his wife. Nothing was going as he expected. It was fast coming to his attention that he didn't know his daughter even in the smallest sense. She wasn't the flighty, fidgety female that he thought her. There was a new serenity about her he wouldn't have thought her ever capable of possessing. It was almost as though she knew something he didn't. The idea was ludicrous but too strong to deny.

Stryker waited, knowing the rest of the family was also waiting to see what Arthur would do and how Tempest would react.

"It's not as if this is a real marriage," Roger murmured uncertainly, his pale brows drawn together as he divided his glance between his uncharacteristically silent father and his volatile sister.

"It's real, Rog." Tempest leaned her head against Stryker's shoulder.

"Don't call me Rog. You know I hate that."

Tempest looked at her brother, her whole family, each in turn, ending with her father. He always led the pack, made the rules, punished the transgressor of those rules with silence or soft, slicing criticism depending on the severity of the mistake. She had feared those moments, she realized, hating them yet oddly courting them, too. But now, she felt neither need. She didn't want to hurt anyone, fight with anyone, but some words just had to be said. It was time and she was strong enough to take the first step out of the cage that Stryker had helped her unlock.

"And I hate being talked down to. Do you know that not one of you has offered us the slightest encouragement, something our butler managed to do the second we set foot in the door?" She looked at each member, her glance lingering just long enough to make her point. For the first time in her life she wasn't allowing her anger and frustration to drive her words. She was calm, really calm. She squeezed Stryker's arm, silently thanking him for the insight he had given her when she needed it the most.

"I don't think anyone meant to upset you, dear," Charlotte King said, speaking for the first time.

"I agree. I don't think any of you *meant* to upset me but until today you always managed it very well. But no more. The how we got married is no one's business but ours. The same with how we stay married."

"Look here, young lady. You will not speak to your mother or to any of us this way. We're your family."

"A family I've spent years trying to live up to. I love you but not enough to keep killing myself to be something that I will never be. I'm different. I admit it. And I'm tired of fighting with you. Love me if you can but stop trying to cram me into a mold that only works for you."

"Tempest!"

"Temp!"

"Young lady, you will not forget who you are."

Only Roger abstained from jumping at the challenge Tempest had issued.

Stryker rose, saying nothing as he held out his hand to his wife.

Tempest took it, no longer smiling but equally not drowning from the weight of responsibility that had been slowly dragging her to the bottom of her own emotional pool. They walked to the door, side by side.

Arthur took a single step toward them, then stopped. "Stryker. You won't leave like this."

Stryker turned then, eyeing his boss. "Orders, Arthur. That only works at the office."

Arthur scowled, angered but trying to hold it in. He couldn't afford to lose Stryker's skill. He knew very well that any number of companies envied him his troubleshooter and quite a few had even had the guts to attempt to hire him away from Whitney-King International. Stryker could leave his company tomorrow and be on the job with an organization just as influential and with a salary just as lucrative as his current one.

"We have to talk." Arthur spread his hands, seeking but not finding a way to reach Stryker and his daughter.

"Not like this. You've spent years sending me off to take care of your daughter. I've done it, for you, for her, and because I cared about her. I always thought you did, too. Now, I'm not so sure." He looked down at the silent woman who guarded his side, who had watched over him in the jungle as he had slept the sleep of the exhausted, who had followed where he led without a complaint in spite of a fever that was draining the last ounces of her strength. "She is my wife, my responsibility. Both I accept without reservation. What I won't accept is someone, anyone hurting her."

Arthur opened his mouth for rebuttal, but his wife's hand on his arm stopped him in midbreath.

"Will you stay for lunch? Cook has made Tempest's favorite dessert and all of us would like to hear about your adventures and the island." She rose, the slender woman with the physical look of her youngest daughter but without the take-it-on-the-chin gleam in her light blue eyes.

Stryker looked down at Tempest, seeing her stare wistfully at her mother. "We'd like that." He smiled at the woman he had never seen go against her husband. Maybe he had underestimated her role. Maybe Tempest had an ally that neither of them had suspected.

"You're very quiet," Stryker said as he slipped his arms around Tempest's waist and drew her close.

They stood in the small foyer of his apartment. The air had the scent and feel of a long closed up space. The rooms beyond were spacious and sunny when the blinds weren't drawn. Right now they were dark and vaguely gloomy. Neither noticed.

"In all the years I've been aware of what a burden I was to everyone, I've never seen or heard my mother take up for me," she replied by way of an explanation. She leaned into his strength, accepting it, drawing from it, and returning his gift with the warmth of her touch and the surrender that was complete without diminishing her own power.

"You aren't the only one who got a shock," he reminded her.

She smiled faintly. "No. My father looked as if one of his mail clerks had fired everyone in the company from the CEO on down."

"Roger and Lavendar didn't do any better."

Her smile deepened, becoming a soft laugh to banish the lingering remnants of hurt the familial interview had created. Stryker bent his head, her lips too tempting an invitation to resist. She met him with the same eagerness, her hands sliding into the buttons of his shirt, opening them so that his flesh brushed the soft cotton of her dress. He nudged her hips, rotating her body into his so that she could feel the power she had to command his desire. Her soft indrawn breath was a goad and a reward for the tactic.

"The beds aren't made," he whispered.

"I won't notice." She wrapped her arms around his neck. "Carry me."

"I thought you'd never ask."

Stryker came awake by degrees, first conscious of the warm weight of Tempest against his side, then of the satin quilting of the bare mattress beneath his back and the coolness of the room now that the air-conditioner was bringing the temperature down. He eased out of the bed, halting when Tempest muttered in protest at losing her resting place and the heat of his body. He smiled tenderly as he slipped out of her arms and tucked a pillow where his body had lain and then drew the satin comforter up to her waist. The flames of her hair spread over the cream pillow ticking and across her bare breasts. His gaze lingered on the rosy tips for an instant before he covered her completely with the chocolate spread. She muttered once more, then settled with a sigh.

He put on his slacks but left off the shirt before padding through the apartment to the kitchen. A survey of the refrigerator and pantry was just as depressing as he expected. If he had thought to notify his cleaning service, things would have been different, but by the time he had remembered, they had been on the last leg of their flight home.

"Oh, well, there is always takeout," he mumbled, digging into the drawer closest to the phone for the list of places he patronized that delivered. He wanted something special for this first night here. It took only a few minutes to order what he wanted. He went back to check on Tempest. Finding her still asleep, he wandered through the apartment, looking at it from a woman's point of view. He was frowning at the impersonality of the living room when he realized he wasn't alone. He turned to discover Tempest standing in the hall, wrapped in his robe, her eyes curious and faintly anxious.

"What's wrong?"

He came to her, kissing her before dropping an arm over her shoulders. "I was just thinking that this place won't do at all. It worked when there was just me but now there is us."

"It's not so bad."

He flicked her nose as he pulled her down beside him on the couch. "You haven't looked. I've been in better hotel rooms."

Tempest glanced around, wrinkling her nose as she realized the description was apt. "So, let's get a new place. Money isn't exactly a problem." She caught the tail end of his frown. Thinking she knew the hang-up, she added, "I wasn't talking about my money, although you must know anything I have is yours."

"We haven't talked about it, you know."

"It wasn't important," she returned swiftly, disturbed by the strange look in his eyes. "I suppose that's easy to say because I've always known that I could buy almost anything I could possibly want in material stuff. But I've never cared.''

He stopped her words by placing his fingers over her lips. "I know that. I've seen you set up all sorts of charities with your inheritance. I know you're just as comfortable in designer clothes as rough cottons and I have never seen you use the power of your family for anything but good. That wasn't what I meant anyway.''

"Then what did you mean?''

"Nothing more complex than I wanted to find out what kind of house or apartment you wanted. If you wanted children. How you wanted to live. Simple things really.''

"Children?'' she said, staring at him, realizing that she had never given the idea the least consideration. Because of the inherent dangers in her lifestyle, she had been on the Pill for a number of years.

"Doesn't work with your globe trotting, does it?''

She studied his expression, nothing in it to give her a clue as to what he wanted. She had always thought she had courage, but faced with that calm wall that showed no hint of his feelings, she hesitated to ask outright. "I hadn't thought about it,'' she admitted finally, carefully.

"I don't suppose there is any rush, but until we do decide what kind of life we'll have, we can't make any real decisions on new living quarters.''

The doorbell sounded. Startled at the intrusion, Tempest asked, "Visitors?''

"Supper.'' Stryker rose and went to answer.

Tempest listened to the male voices in the hall

without really hearing them. Her thoughts were centered on the sudden problems looming on her horizon. Why hadn't she thought of what being married would mean? She wasn't stupid but in this case it would seem she was guilty of being willfully blind. She knew the kind of value Stryker placed on home and family. She had met Slater and his father and heard enough about the madcap professor Sloane that she shouldn't have been surprised at Stryker's bringing up children. And a house. The decorator's delight she had grown up in was hardly a recommendation for a home, and in consequence she had never bothered to find an apartment of her own for her brief stays in the city. She literally lived out of a suitcase. She had never shopped for a piece of furniture or a rug.

"Now you're frowning," Stryker observed as he came into the living room carrying a large stack of white boxes.

Tempest cleared the coffee table in front of her of the few business magazines. "I was thinking about what you said," she murmured, watching as he set out the food. The fragrance drifting up from the array of containers should have piqued the most jaded palate. This time she was immune.

Stryker glanced at her, reading the confusion and uncertainty in her eyes. But there was no panic, no hint that she was feeling trapped by the questions he had laid before her. He breathed a mental sigh of relief. He hadn't thought about what he had said. If he had, he might have avoided the discussion altogether.

"Want to elaborate?" he asked as he handed her a plate.

"I hadn't thought about a family."

He concentrated on serving his food and keeping his voice as neutral as possible. "Are you against having children?"

Tempest willed him to look at her. She wanted to scream in frustration when he didn't. "I don't think I'd make a very good mother," she said finally.

"Why?"

"The traveling for one."

"A gypsy who always brings presents and exciting stories home is a wonderful being to the very young."

"But if he was sick, I wouldn't be there. Or afraid. Or hurt."

"But I would. And we can find a good nanny to be here when I can't be."

Without realizing it, she filled her plate. "It isn't right."

"By normal standards perhaps not. But I thought we agreed to make our own rules." He looked at her then, challenging her.

Tempest's chin came up, the worry in her eyes changing in a blink to a dare accepted. "We did."

"Then the question really is whether you want children, not how we will take care of them."

She thought for a moment. It was all too easy to see a miniature of Stryker, dark hair, intense dark eyes, a sturdy body, and a mind that would run rings around any nanny. She thought of her features, her hair on a small being, the kind of scrapes a child with an inquisitive mind could get into. The picture was strangely bewitching and at the same time awesomely frightening.

Stryker set his plate on the table and framed her face with his hands. "Tell me what you're thinking."

"I do want children," she confessed, as surprised as he by the words she hadn't known hovered on her tongue.

He kissed her softly, teasing her lips, tasting her agreement, and finding it good. "Then we'll need a house," he said as he raised his head. "Something with a fenced yard and places for children to run and play."

"So easy?"

He shook his head. "We both know it won't be. But we're in this together. We'll make it work."

"I've never run a house."

"We'll hire a good housekeeper." He kissed her forehead before he released her. "I can afford it."

"No, I'll hire the housekeeper and the nanny since it's my jobs they'll be doing." She waited for an argument. She received a grin and a nod.

"Sounds fair."

Her brows rose. "You aren't going to beat your chest and claim male pride over . . ." She halted, unprepared to say "my money" again.

"No." He cut into the succulent steak that had been cooked just the way he liked it. "We're equals. I can't match you in dollars but that's the only place that our team isn't pulling even. I trust you not to rub my nose in your millions. Just as you trust me not to tie you into the traditional role of wife and woman. Fair trade, I think."

"A lot of men wouldn't see it that way." She took a bite of her own steak.

"I'm not a lot of men any more than you are a lot of women."

The perfect answer, Tempest decided, smiling. She leaned across, took the fork he had halfway to his mouth, and kissed him as tenderly as he had ever kissed her. "I like the way you think, my husband."

His eyes glittered with something more complicated than pleasure and more simple than passion. "Only the way I think?"

She laughed, poked his fork back in his hand, and returned to her dinner. "For now. Maybe later I'll change my mind."

ELEVEN

"This sounds good." Tempest pointed to the small real estate ad in the newspaper as she read aloud. "Two-story home with pool on twenty acres with a five-horse barn, cross fencing, woods, and stream. Gardens and security system. Six bedrooms, four baths, six thousand square feet in the main house, and a guest cottage with two bedrooms and one bath." She wiggled around on Stryker's lap, pushing the paper out of the way. "That's the best of the lot this morning. You know it is. It has the land you said you liked, the bedrooms I wanted, and guest quarters for when your brothers and father visit. And even stables. What more can you ask?"

His lips twitched at her blatant angling. "Honey, a reasonable price tag would be nice."

"You know very well it won't be too bad. We're still trying to come out of our slump from when the oil industry crashed. Bet we can get it at a giveaway cost."

"You wouldn't know a giveaway price if you fell over it."

She kissed him, a teasing smack that made him laugh. She couldn't remember a time she had been so content, so happy. They had awakened wrapped in each other's arms. They had made love as the sun had filled the room with gold shadows and rivers of white light. They had showered, playing and loving, and then gone on a culinary treasure hunt in the pantry for a tin of coffee Stryker had insisted was his private store for mornings when he had forgotten to tell the cleaning service to fill his larder. They had found it in a dark corner. There wasn't any cream but they did have sugar. While the coffee was brewing, Stryker had gone down to the corner and bought a newspaper. So far they had perused every ad, discarded all but three and this last one, and consumed the entire pot of coffee.

"Don't go to sleep on me," Stryker teased, hugging her.

"I love you," she said suddenly, no longer laughing.

His amusement flickered, a bright light entering his eyes at the depth that hadn't been there even in the throes of their morning passion. Every instinct went on alert. She was changing from moment to moment. He had never seen her so relaxed, so at peace. He wanted to ask what was happening to her. He had a hunch, but he desperately wanted to be sure. Instead, he listened to his instincts, corralling his need to get into her thought and relying on patience developed in his work to play it light, to allow Tempest to come to him, to reach for him with more than her passion and her love. It was more difficult than anything he had attempted. "That makes it nice. I love you, too."

Disappointment slipped through the contentment. She felt cheated at the gentle, clearly sincere words that didn't carry the power she suddenly needed. Confused, knowing very well that his open hands that allowed her the freedom she always needed were the only reason she had consented to this marriage, Tempest fought the strange reaction, seeking to hide it from him and forget it herself. She didn't succeed in either case. If she had waited for Stryker to say something to her, she waited in vain. He simply leaned past her and picked up the paper to scan the ad again.

"Maybe you're right. If this looks as good as it sounds, then it just might do." He folded the paper and rose with her in his arms. "Ready to go house hunting?"

"Yes, let's," she agreed, suddenly needing to escape the confines of the apartment. Only this time she knew that her escape wouldn't bring her the sense of freedom that had always followed her. Rather this time she was running from herself and that couldn't be done.

Tempest stared at the house set on the small hill. In a state that held trees at a premium, the mini-estate had more than its share. There were woods, obviously planted and tended by man's hand rather than nature's. The main house itself was of natural rock, yet gracefully designed for all its more rough-hewn materials. Glass shone in the sunlight, reflecting the earth, trees, and sky in one-dimensional detail. The stable area was set well away from the central structure, and the guest cottage was in the opposite direction, connected by a path to the house and surrounded by its own small territory of flowers and trees. The whole effect was cool in the Texas heat, lush beauty, and privacy. Tempest fell in love with it.

"Tell me you like it," she commanded, turning to Stryker, her emotions as clear as a snow-fed mountain stream.

Stryker threaded his fingers with hers, grinning at her eagerness. "It looks good on the outside," he agreed with deliberate blandness.

She pouted at him, something she had never done in her life. In that moment, had she known it, she looked as carefree and as well loved as any woman truly beloved of her husband. "I'll work my fingers to the bone if the inside needs help. I promise. Say that we can have it."

He shook his head, teasing her. "I'm not promising anything." Urging her up the steps to the entrance, he ignored her mumbled rebuttal.

"I'll make it worth your while," she suggested, putting every bit of seldom used feminine guile into her voice.

He stopped, turned, and looked her up and down, much as a trainer would inspect a horse before a race. "Now that is a thought," he murmured roughly, his body reacting instantly to all sorts of images that had plagued him for years. He glanced at the house as though debating the situation. Before he could come to a conclusion, the door opened to a smiling real estate agent.

"Isn't it a wonderful house and so close to the city?" The woman stepped back for them to enter.

Tempest tried to look unimpressed. It wasn't that the house was more beautifully appointed than any she had seen. It wasn't. Nor was it the largest or the most expensive. It was simply that something about it demanded that she and Stryker live there, that they could be happy within these walls and on these grounds. She had never known such a feeling of homecoming. As they followed the agent, Emma West, from room to room, she kept waiting for the feeling to wane. It didn't. It grew in intensity as the interior proved to be as delightful as the exterior. She tried to read Stryker's face as he questioned Emma about various aspects of the property. No hint of his thinking betrayed him; no glance told her that he was as determined to have this house as she was becoming. Restless, wanting to just make an offer and secure their home, Tempest tried to be as cool as he, at least until they were alone, something that didn't happen until Emma's beeper called her to her car phone, leaving them in the shadowy privacy of the barn.

"Well?" she demanded.

"I like it."

It took a second for his words to sink in, and when they did, she launched herself against him, kissing him excitedly. Stryker caught her close, laughing at her delight, sharing it, and hoping for more in the future. That Tempest was so intent on making a home with him instead of simply sharing an apartment was more than he expected. When she finally let him breathe, he added carefully, watching her reaction, "Are you really sure you want this house?" He covered her mouth with his hands before she could give an impulsive decision she could regret. "This kind of place, even with a staff, isn't going to be something I can handle for long periods of time and still do my job, especially if we have a child."

"Oh!" She considered the situation, realizing that he was right. She looked past him to the house that seemed to be sleeping, an architectural beauty, waiting for its prince and, in this case, princess to awaken it. "You and I have been together now for a few weeks and I haven't felt the need to take off," she said slowly. "That's the longest I've been in one place in years."

"Novelty?"

She didn't lie. "Maybe. But it doesn't feel like it." She searched his face, reading curiosity but nothing more in his expression. Disappointed without understanding why, she continued, "When I'm with you, I feel complete. I don't feel the need to run." She shrugged, not certain she wasn't being too honest. She couldn't remember ever making herself this vulnerable to anyone.

Stryker hadn't believed he could be fool enough to hope she would settle with him. He had truly thought when he had almost forced her into marriage that he had accepted her will-o'-the-wisp nature. In that moment, he learned differently. Hope unfurled its tender shoots in his heart. He wanted to demand more from her. The urge was swift, almost too strong for his control. He hung on, knowing that if he rushed her, if he tried in any way to cage her, he would lose. She was circling, his eagle, choosing her nest and her mate. He had to allow her that freedom, although every nerve in him screamed that he tie her to him with unbreakable bonds.

"I want to try." She stroked his jaw, her eyes holding his. "I don't want to leave you," she admitted huskily. "Not for a night or a day. I've never felt like this before. I'm terrified this peace won't last. But I want it, too." She buried her face in the hollow of his neck. "Oh, I want it, too."

He held her tight, staring over her head into a future he hadn't believed would ever be his. He would buy a hundred houses if it would keep her with him every night and every day. He would move mountains, fight her family and anyone else for that chance. His eyes darkened with purpose, hope, and a fear as great as hers. Their marriage bargain had a new set of rules and he intended to do his best with them. If Tempest was truly trying to nest, he would be there. His life with her depended on his ability to solve problems and to have patience while she found her place in their life. He was her anchor. Out of all the uncertainty of the future, he understood that very well.

"We'll take the house."

She raised her head. "You won't regret it," she promised. His smile was a warm bath of love. She sank into it, relaxing as she had never dared before.

"You've never broken a promise to me." He leaned down, his lips hovering an inch from hers. Her breath was warm, mating with his.

"I won't break this one." She pulled his head the

rest of the way down until their lips married, his breath to hers, his taste, his strength, hers. So many facets, so many sensations, so many possibilities for happiness. Freedom. It was Stryker, the joy she found in his arms, the love she saw in his dark eyes. Her husband.

"Oops, I'm sorry."

Tempest and Stryker broke apart at the sheepish apology. Emma stood in the doorway, smiling, looking as if she wasn't certain whether she should go away and come back. Tempest stepped out of Stryker's arms, laughing. "We're sort of on our honeymoon," she said.

Emma grinned. "That explains it then."

Humor at the situation and plain old-fashioned happiness flashed in Stryker's eyes as he took Tempest's arm and urged her out of the barn. "About the house?"

Emma looked from one to the other. Only Tempest's face showed her feelings but it was enough. "You want it." She looked at the property, one she had always liked even though it was too big for most people. "I'm glad. I've shown this house so many times since it came on our list. It's a beautiful place but more than most can handle."

"We'll make an offer," he said, then named the figure.

Emma frowned. "That's a good deal less than we're asking."

"I saw the date it came on the market in the listing book. There hasn't been a price reduction. And as you said, it isn't the type of place that everyone can afford."

Respect glittered in Emma's eyes as she shook her head. "I had a feeling you were going to be tough."

Tempest leaned her head against Stryker's shoulder, content to let him do the bargaining. She knew in her bones the house would be theirs. She said as much when they were on their way back to Stryker's apartment after leaving Emma with the offer and a promise to call them as soon as she contacted and received word from the owners.

"I think we can get it too. Things are going to be tight for a while, so don't get any ideas about going crazy with redecorating." He slanted her a glance, catching the beginnings of the smug look on her face. "I don't like that expression. What are you plotting?"

"Well, since you are buying the house, I thought you might like me to outfit the stables and get the furniture. This kind of place is going to need a lot of stuff. As for the redecorating, I know a woman who's especially good at making a home rather than furnishing a house."

Once more Tempest was showing him how involved she intended to be on the home front. He would agree to anything that brought her closer. "All right. Sounds fair. But I warn you, I hate stiff furniture. You aren't thinking of putting pieces in that no one can sit on, are you?"

She laughed. "No. In fact, I'm dragging you with me when we shop."

He groaned, not meaning a word of it, but husbandly prerogative had to be upheld. "How long?"

"Weeks if we're lucky," she replied cheerfully, ideas already doing a war dance in her mind. She could see a lovely cherry wood dining set. Soft couches and lots of pillows in the upstairs sitting room. His furniture in the bedroom. So many plans, so much work, and she couldn't wait to get started.

Jonathan Marchant eyed the address written in his secretary's precise hand and compared it with the address on the stylish high-rise apartment building across the street from his parking place. He had found the McGuires. Collecting his briefcase, he got out of the car, glanced down at the knife creases in his pants, and smoothed his jacket carefully so that no hint of travel disarray would show. He wasn't a man who handled sloppiness in any form. As he walked methodically across the street, a car came past him, two occupants smiling, talking. The quick glimpse he had of the young woman in the passenger seat told him that his arrival had been perfectly timed. The McGuires had been out and now were returning. He allowed himself one small smile as he entered the lobby and waited. A few minutes later, he got his first live look at the man Tempest Whitney had chosen to marry her granddaughter. Without realizing it, he relaxed slightly as he approached the couple. Tempest saw him first.

"Marchie," Tempest said, smiling, her head tipped to one side curiously. "What are you doing here?"

Jonathan grimaced at the nickname Tempest had given him when she had been a precocious six. It had stuck all these years in spite of his attempts, halfhearted although he would never admit it, to change it. "Meeting your new husband," he murmured, extending his hand and introducing himself.

"And begging a little of your time on a matter for your grandmother."

Tempest frowned, her hand tightening in Stryker's. "My grandmother?"

After a quick look at the older man's face, Stryker headed for the elevators. "Not here, honey." Whatever had brought old Miss Tempest's pet legal beagle hunting them, it was something that had the man rattled. He sighed soundlessly, glad his life before Tempest had been built on handling crises. He wouldn't have wanted to tackle living with her from the basis of a normal nine-to-five existence. He wouldn't have made it past the first day.

The elevator doors swished closed. "She's been gone for four years," Tempest said, frowning.

Jonathan sighed deeply and took a better grip on his case. "I know. I was beginning to think I would have to wait five more years to discharge my final obligation to her."

They stepped out of the compartment in single file and entered Stryker's apartment the same way. Tempest tucked her arm in Jonathan's and led him to the couch. "You're being cryptic. You know I hate that."

The lawyer sat down and opened his briefcase to extract three sheaths of papers. He handed one each to Stryker and Tempest and kept one for himself. "I am not good with words. Never have been. Leave that kind of thing for my partners. But I draw an ironclad contract. You're looking at one of my works. I don't like what I did. I won't lie to you about that. But your grandmother, Tempest, was not a woman a man could deny when she set her mind on something. For all her softness she had steel to her backbone when it came to you and your happiness." He reached in his case and took out two letters, again giving one to each of them. "She asked if you would both read these before I explained what's in the legal trash you hold . . ." He grimaced eloquently. ". . . her words, not mine, believe me."

Tempest looked at Stryker, easily reading a confusion that matched her own. "I don't understand any of this," she murmured, oddly reluctant to open the envelope that bore her name in the elegant script of her beloved grandmother.

"She loved you. Whatever is in here was for you," Stryker said quietly before slitting his own envelope and pulling out the stationery it contained. He waited until Tempest had done the same before reading the words flowing before him. His brows rose from the end of the first sentence. Every vestige of emotion had fled his expression by the time he was finished. He looked up, straight into Tempest's stunned eyes.

"I don't know what to say. I don't want it. It should belong to you. Twenty-seven million dollars."

Jonathan permitted himself a grunt that could have meant anything as he studied Stryker, accurately reading the sincerity and shock in his eyes. He knew of the man from the reports he had had prepared after the elder Tempest had died. Such an investigation had been outside his scope as a lawyer, but his allegiance to both Tempests had demanded that he be certain of the man who meant so much to both for such different reasons. He had been impressed by what he had found. Nothing he had heard or discovered since had changed his mind.

"She was quite clear on her bequest. The will is unbreakable. I won't tell you you couldn't try to overturn it but you won't. She left you her fortune, a fortune aside from the millions her only son had inherited on his father's death. This was her private money, a gift from her own grandmother. I've been holding it in trust for you. If you had not married Tempest by the time you were forty, it would have come to you anyway. She felt that you should have it, for out of all her family and the Kings, you were the only one who never gave up or walked away from her granddaughter. She said it wasn't a reward for services rendered. Nothing, no dollar amount could ever be high enough for the times you had rescued Tempest, or the risks you had taken. She wanted you to think of it as a gift of love from an old lady who cared more for her namesake than she had ever loved anyone on this earth."

He looked at Tempest. "And for you, she wanted to give Stryker an even footing with you if you did marry. She knew him well enough, she said, that she didn't think he would care about the difference between your economic states. But she wanted to ensure there would never be a question in anyone's mind that money was his goal in marrying you. She said she knew your heart even if you didn't know it yourself. She always said that one day you two would marry. She believed in you. She wanted what was best." He spread his hands, dividing his glance between them. "I tried to talk her out of this extraordinary course. But she was adamant. You, Mr.

McGuire, get every penny of her cash assets. Tempest receives the house, the furnishings, and all the land and her grandmother's personal effects and jewelry.''

"I don't want this," Stryker repeated, speaking directly to the lawyer. "Deed it over to Tempest."

Tempest's vehement negative was overridden by Jonathan's no.

"It can't be done. If you attempt such a course, the whole, Tempest's part and yours is divided into various trusts. On your death, even then she only inherits if there are no children of the union. Otherwise the money is in trust for your offspring." He studied Stryker's face. "She was in her right mind."

Tempest slid her hand into Stryker's. "Don't fight her, darling," she said gently, looking into his turbulent eyes. "I am happy with what she has done. Don't you see? I have spent my life fighting the opinion of others. In one stroke grandmother has saved us both from that. We know why we married but think how much easier it will be when this gets out. You would have been wealthy no matter what. In fact, I think right now I could easily be marrying you for your money. I don't think I'm worth twenty-seven million on my best day."

Stryker touched her cheek, searching her eyes for the honesty she had always given him. "Are you sure? I don't need this. Hell, I'm not even sure what to do with it since I apparently have to take it or deprive you of your half."

She carried his hand to her lips, kissing his palm. "If it really bothers you, let the whole mess go to charity. I can live with that."

"You're sure?"

She smiled as she kissed his palm again. "Yes. Almost as sure as I am that I love you."

Holding her hand, Stryker considered the future, the freedom that would be his, not being on call for Whitney-King. He could raise their children, fly with Tempest, have the resources and time to rescue her if it became necessary. So many benefits that far exceeded the actual dollar count. So many problems solved by a loving lady who cared about Tempest for her own sake. He could not betray that love by refusing. He focused on the lawyer. "All right. I'll take it. Now, what?"

Jonathan smiled restrainedly. He wasn't a man given to showing his emotions, but for a moment there, he had been certain that Tempest Whitney had made one of her rare errors in judgment. She had warned him Stryker would fight the inheritance, but she had been positive the thought of cheating Tempest out of anything would save the day. She had been right. He wished she were alive right now so that he could tell her so.

"Now, you will read the will. Sign a number of papers and take over Miss Tempest's holdings so that I can finally retire in peace." Tempest's laugh startled him.

"Marchie, you made a joke."

His brows raised. "I never joke."

Tempest giggled as she opened her grandmother's will. "It sure sounded like a joke to me."

Jonathan glanced down at the first page of the testament. "I certainly hope marriage settles you down, my dear. Your grandmother assured me that it would be just the thing for you.''

Tempest tossed her head, her red hair flashing fire in the sunlight pouring through the windows. "If you tell me she thought marriage to Stryker would settle me, I won't believe you.''

"No. She never said that, although I asked her." He looked up, his frown deepening in bewilderment. "All she said was that if you had the good sense to march Stryker down the aisle that she would know you had found yourself at last, even if it took you a while to realize it yourself.''

Stryker tipped back his head, laughing before he could stifle the urge. He had always enjoyed the surprisingly tart-tongued older Tempest the few times he had seen her. She knew her granddaughter and loved her unreservedly. Those two things alone had always commanded his respect and caring. Now, it seemed Tempest senior had clear-sightedness he hadn't credited. For the first time since Jonathan had announced his extraordinary mission he relaxed. Being mega-wealthy held little interest for him, but clearing his future with Tempest of obstacles and barriers did. If the older Tempest had been present in the room, he would have shocked the assembled company by lifting the spry little lady in his arms and kissing her soundly.

TWELVE

Stryker stood at the window, his back to the room that Tempest had created for him at the rear of their new house. The view was something special, a survey of man's domain, the trees, the pastures, the barn, the beauty of this land that now bore his and Tempest's name. He should have been content. The decorator that Tempest had hired to help with the furnishing of the house had departed last week when the final work had been completed. Tempest and she had done a wonderful job. The rooms were gracious, spacious, and light filled without having the impersonal perfection of so many of the larger homes that he had visited. Tempest's nest had truly become a home in the short weeks of their occupation.

He shrugged broad shoulders, restless, disturbed, and knowing that contentment had never been farther away. Tempest was still loving, as generous and as impulsively affectionate as ever. But she was no longer with him in mind and body. Her movements betrayed her, although, as yet, she had said nothing to indicate that she was fighting her own instincts to fly. In fact, just the opposite was occurring. She was throwing herself feverishly into any activity he suggested, be it riding at dawn or walking in the moonlight. He had taken her to town, dining and dancing. They had visited her family and even Slater and Joy had made the trip over to see them for a few days. Both his efforts and hers had been futile. The chains of domesticity were beginning to bind. Tempest was fluttering her wings, testing the air for flight. He looked across the yard as she came out of the barn, leading the stallion that only an experienced rider would have dared to mount, much less ride at breakneck speed. The steel-gray horse reared, pawing at the sky, fighting the bit and the woman who had the courage and skill to meet him on his own turf and win his obedience.

Stryker's hands tightened on the sill as he watched the strangely equal duel of wills. He had wanted to ask her not to buy that stud, but he had said nothing even when he read the waiting challenge in her eyes. The gray was a test, unconscious perhaps, on Tempest's part but a test nonetheless. She was waiting for the ax to fall, for him to turn into her overprotective and demanding family. So he had swallowed his fear, looked her in the eye, and agreed to the stallion. He rode with her, watching the way the rogue fought, and still he said nothing. He had nightmares about the horse and Tempest lying hurt and bleeding somewhere in the hot Texas sun. He accepted the fear and the nightmares. He had no choice, for he had forfeited the right when he had taken her as his wife. He had made her his promise and he had kept it. But it wasn't enough to hold her close.

Stryker watched her bring the stallion onto all fours, her hair bright flames in the sunlight as she tossed her head, laughing with the rush of power that besting the animal had given her. Then she set him free, bending low over the muscled neck, probably shouting into the flattened ears to fly. Both woman and horse hurtled out of the yard, a living streak of energy barely under control. He turned from the scene, hurting in ways against which he had no defense. He walked to the desk, sat down, feeling years older for every minute Tempest chased the horizon, following the needs that drove her to risk life and limb in a search without a name. Reaching into the drawer on his right, he took out the envelope that Jonathan Marchant had given him over two and a half months before. He knew the words by heart. Sometimes, when the hell of loving Tempest was almost too great to be borne, he held onto the only hope that seemed to remain. Her namesake's words.

One of the things I have always admired about you, Stryker, was your honesty, self and with others. You have seen my granddaughter as, I suspect, no one knows her. You, out of all of us, all those years ago, knew to ask if she had done that thing at school. You, out of all of us, cared enough about her to teach her how to take care of herself instead of just demanding that she give up a life that she clearly could not forfeit. You have been the truest of us, loving her, protecting her when she would allow you, and often, I think, when she fought you every inch of the way and rescuing her when no one else could have. For this I love you. You have saved my granddaughter. Jonny will have told you why I leave you the money. I know you don't need it and won't want it. You are a man who will always make his way. But I would give you what you have always given my granddaughter, freedom. I don't know what the future will be. If you are indeed married, I pray for you and her. She doesn't know herself, only what others think of her. She fights, so hard, blindly because no one was there when it could have made a difference to help her see. I love my son but he has no give in him, and that clutch of children and his wife are too well molded by him to matter.

Life is too short for regrets but if I allowed myself one it is that, I fear, you met my Tempest too late. Now, what you might have shown her, helped her learn, she must learn herself. But the instinct to fight is so finely developed, the paths of escape so well traveled that she may not see. I pray I am wrong. My only hope is the man you are, patient, strong enough to hold onto her without her knowing, loving her until she can love herself and accept the fullness of the woman she can be. Then she will come home to you to stay. And you will have won. Not with emotional chains, demands, and guilts but with the pure love that none of us, myself included, has ever been able to give her.

"I hope you're right, Miss Tempest. I watch her chafe at the routine and I feel her need to run."

Despair laced his words, worry carved new lines in his face. Endurance was a costly virtue. He paid. But not alone. Tempest was paying too, a greater price perhaps than his own. She was fighting for them, alone, shadows she would not share with him. If he needed a measure of her love, he found it in the circles that were beginning to show beneath her now clouded eyes. He felt it in the desperation of her lovemaking, her frenetic energy, her determination to submerge herself in their life. He saw it in the wild rides that he knew were her substitute for the life she was determined to renounce.

"I want to help her but there isn't a damn thing I can do," he muttered, thrusting the stationery back into its envelope and slamming the drawer. He reached for the phone. He had a number of calls to make. Since he had quit Whitney-King to take over administration of his inheritance, he was busier than he had ever been. The work was challenging, demanding, and intricate enough to more than compensate for the change in his life-style. If Tempest had been happy, he would have needed nothing else. His life was filled with more than he had ever hoped, enough for a future many times over.

Tempest reined the stallion in at the edge of their land. He fought the bit for a moment, snorting and throwing his head so that his mane lashed at her like whips. She laughed, swaying in the saddle slightly so the long strands couldn't connect.

"Monster," she chided cheerfully, patting the

arching neck as she urged him into a restrained canter. He hated the gait, his favorite being a wild gallop. But for today, this moment, she needed to think.

Dan's call. She should have told Stryker about it. She had certainly had the opportunity. Better still she should have refused to even consider the idea her old friend had outlined. A kayak trip down a relatively unknown river in Indonesia was no one's idea of an easy journey. There were only about a hundred miles of workable water and that boasted waterfalls and at least one six-rated white water stretch. It would take days to negotiate the length. She would be the only woman among five others, four of them men she had run white water with before, men she trusted and who trusted her. But no matter how she cut it, the trip was dangerous, more dangerous perhaps than anything she had tried to date. Three months ago she wouldn't have hesitated. She would have packed her boat and gear and been ready before the rest of the team. But no longer. She wanted to go. She knew that, expected it, but what she hadn't expected was the strange need to stay that suddenly was almost as strong as the urge to soar on this next challenge. She should have told Stryker. He had promised her freedom. She knew he wouldn't like the party, but he had promised not to stop her when she needed to go. And Stryker always kept his promises.

So what was her problem? Why couldn't she just tell him about the trip, accept his presence, and pack? With the money Grandmother had left him, they didn't have to even worry about working it into his schedule. He was as free as she to come and go.

Without realizing, Tempest drew to a stop, her eyes staring at the horizon she no longer saw.

"I have to tell him," she whispered. "He loves me. He understands." She heard the plea in her own voice with a sense of shock. Tears pooled in her eyes. He would understand and he would let her go but she would know it was only because he had promised he would release her. Her family had always used their love as a chain to try to shackle her to the life they thought was best. She had vowed she would never do that to herself or any other. But she had. In her arrogance, her need to be free, she had bound Stryker to a world that he endured for her sake and hers alone. He loved her. To her soul and back she knew that. And because he loved her, he knew that she was fighting just as he knew that he was hurting because of the restlessness that she couldn't hide. His arms held her when the night was dark, folding in on her, yet she felt secure rather than trapped. His words whispered in the silence, reminding her that she was free. His body offered her temporary amnesia and his silence allowed her to make her own choices. But he would pay for those choices. Whether he went with her or not, he would worry and fear for her safety. He would let her go but she would trap him with that legacy. And therein lay her burden. She hadn't the strength to stay and she condemned him in a hell of her making when she flew toward the sun and her own dreams.

The tears overfilled, sliding down her face, painting grief over the smooth satin skin that his hand had warmed, his lips had traced. For the first time in her life, she faced what she had become and found the image so painful she wanted to turn away from it forever. But how? His arms, his love were strong. But she could not lean, even in this moment of anguish she understood that. To use Stryker and the gift of caring he offered her in this way was to betray them both. Better that she should leave, fly as the unfettered bird she had been than to do that. Wiping the backs of hands against her cheeks, she turned the stallion's head toward home.

She would go but at least she would be honest enough with him to tell him why she did and what it was costing her to leave him. It wouldn't make his burden less but it would allow him to know that she wished she could share the weight of what her decision meant to their life. She rode slowly, her memories vivid of chances taken with a laugh that defied the gods, of challenges bested, of friends gained and lost, of families and their false promises of love that existed only if she was different than she was born. So futile. All of it. What had she gained? Moments of intense living that had fed an addiction for more. Now she was hooked, caught in an infinite loop with no going back. Defeated as she never had been, she entered Stryker's study, closing the door behind her.

He looked up, reading the decision in her face, bracing himself even as he leaned back in a seemingly relaxed sprawl.

"Good ride?"

Tempest took a chair without taking her eyes from Stryker's. "I hate this," she murmured with a depth of sadness she made no attempt to disguise. "No matter what, I love you."

Stryker hurt for her, for the pain he could hear in

her voice, for the anguish he could see in her eyes. He wanted to take her in his arms and promise her anything to make the world right for her again. "Tell me," he invited softly.

She looked down, his tender tone cutting through all her arguments, hurting her more than ever. "Don't be nice to me. I don't deserve it because I'm going. I can't help myself. I want to, but, God help me, I can't stay." She raised her eyes, the tears glittering in the blue depths, her features twisted with the conflict. Stryker half rose, only the sudden protesting slice of her hand stopping him from going to her. "Don't. If you love me, don't touch me right now. I won't be able to finish."

He sank in his chair, waiting, praying now as her grandmother had promised.

"Dan Laurence called three days ago. He's getting up a party to do some white water kayaking."

Stryker almost relaxed. One of Tempest's most developed skills was her ability with the light craft, and she had tried most of the roughest white water in the world and come out on top. And her friend, Dan, was almost as good as Tempest.

"Where?"

Tempest named the river in a quiet voice and waited for the explosion.

Stryker stared at her. He had thought he had seen the worst she could pull, but this idea was past the point of all the other combined. "You mean that hundred miles of water that hasn't been touched by more than a handful of people and only one woman that I know of?"

She nodded, stunned at the neutrality of his voice.

"Dan has been down it?"

"No."

Stryker kept his position by sheer willpower. The urge to get up and shake her until her teeth rattled, to lock her in the house and never allow her out again, was so strong that he just looked at her silently. His promise. It was written in hell and kept there to burn him now in ways that even Satan himself would have denied. "When do you leave?" he asked, every word coming out clearly and distinctly with not one ounce of emotion in a single syllable.

"The charter plane will be here tomorrow." Still, she waited for his demand to accompany her.

"How long will you be gone?"

It was then, staring into those dark eyes, eyes that no longer held any light at all, that she understood the full meaning of his questions. "A couple of weeks." She didn't want to believe what she was thinking. She couldn't believe it. He wouldn't allow her to go alone. Not for this. Not knowing the danger. He was always there, always demanding her caution. But this time, there was no demand, no plea to remain, no controlled impatience, nothing but complete acceptance. The thing she had thought she wanted above even love. Ashes of a dead fire. The knowledge hit her with the force of a perfectly directed attack. "You aren't coming?" she said slowly.

Stryker rose and paced to the window in measured steps. If he looked at her now, he would weaken. He would take back his promise and consign his future instead of himself to hell. "No. Dan is good. He won't do any less about safety precautions than

I would. Besides that, he's the expert there. I don't kayak, if you will recall.''

Tempest stared at his back, lost and not understanding why. ''Ask me to stay,'' she said, the words rushing out of her confusion.

It was his turn to be startled. He swung around, his brows raised, hope rising as a Phoenix from the ashes of his dream. ''What did you say?''

''Ask me to stay.'' She surged to her feet, rushing to his side, fighting to mean the words that now rose like a wave of emotion between them. She caught his hand, a lifeline for her, a link to the future she could see slipping away. ''Tell me I can't go. It's too dangerous.''

He touched the tears flowing down her cheeks with wondering fingers. Her eyes held an anguish to match his own. A strange time for tenderness, but in that moment, it was the only feeling he could be sure of. ''I can't do that. Even for you, I can't do that. Yes, I want you to stay. Yes, I think it's too dangerous even with your skill and the team Dan has undoubtedly put together. But I can't. I won't build our life on asking you for something you can't give. I've watched you try to live this life we're building. It's hurting you. I see you looking out these windows, your eyes yearning for a glimpse of the next horizon. I watch you and that stallion gallop like the wild things you both are over the land, racing the wind and fighting to run even faster, beyond your strengths because the need to challenge yourselves is buried so deep that nothing, no one means as much to you as that killing pace.'' He slipped his hand from her suddenly nerveless grip and brought it to her face.

He cupped her jaw in his palms, staring into her eyes, finding a peace he hadn't known possible.

"Go on your adventure. You want it so badly it's eating you alive. Dance with death and, if God is willing, come back to me." He leaned forward and kissed her forehead. When he raised his head, he even managed a smile that reached his eyes. There was sadness but a knowledge deeper than the universe was wide. "I love you. No matter what, I don't regret marrying you." He slowly released her, his fingers opening as fans as they slid away from her skin. "Go call Dan. I imagine he's waiting on pins at this late date."

Tempest turned, obeying the words because she didn't know what else to do. She felt empty, cut adrift in a world she didn't know. Complete freedom. Stryker loved her enough to give her complete freedom. She made her call in a daze, hardly reacting to Dan's delight or the plans he made to collect her or the impressive list of other kayak enthusiasts who had confirmed. It was a rush to get ready and she never could have done it without Stryker's help. Her boat was collected from her parents' home since it hadn't been moved as yet. Her gear and clothes were packed, traveler's checks purchased. Dinner was spent going over details to make certain she had forgotten nothing.

"I'll do your final check if you want to go on up and get ready for bed," Stryker offered, studying the list of equipment and luggage loaded into the new truck they had purchased the week before.

Tempest stretched tiredly. "It will be faster with two of us."

He glanced at her, shaking his head. "You're beat. I'm not. And even if I were, I can rest tomorrow. You'll be in the air for more hours than you'll want to remember. And you know you wear yourself out in the confinement of flying."

She grimaced, not disputing him. She didn't have the energy or the inclination. "All right." She headed for the door. "I'll wait for you."

Stryker let her go without answering. He simply returned his attention to the last chore remaining before they left in the morning. He didn't think. He knew the time would come when he would but it wasn't now. Less than an hour later, he entered their bedroom, pausing with his back to the closed door, staring at Tempest as she lay asleep, naked, on the bed they shared. She was on her side, her hand outflung as though searching for his warmth. He knew the feeling intimately. Always searching, forever coming up against a cold emptiness that nothing on earth could fill. He shrugged out of his clothes, vowing that tonight, this night alone, he would defy the fates, his own promise, and a soul-deep regret that would come with the dawn. He couldn't ask her to stay. But just maybe he could weave her a dream of passion and silent love that would breach her defenses, slip into her soul, and burn out forever the restlessness that condemned them both. He slid into bed, easing his arms under her, listening to her soft sigh of contentment, feeling the way she curled into his heat, her body automatically adjusting to his.

He started at her hairline, his fingers tracing every curve, the tiny blue veins at her temples, the bright fans of her lashes, her cheek, her lips. His kisses trailed his tactile exploration, breathing warmth over her flesh, touching nerves so that she murmured drowsily but didn't wake to break the spell he was casting. His hands drifted lower, adoring, paying homage to the body he treasured and she took for granted, her long limbs, the sleek muscles that held such strength, the delicate bones that could brave all life had to offer and still demand more, the feet that would carry her from him in the morning, the ankle she had broken one dark stormy night. With each stroke, Tempest's body yielded more completely to him, flowing like priceless silk in his arms, bending to his will, his chained need. He smiled at her pleasure, still not seeking her passion. He wanted the fire but he needed the possession of her soul and heart more. He bent to her lips, his tongue outlining the fullness of each half. Her breath whispered in a sigh of need. He sampled it, teasing her so that her mouth parted gently, seeking blindly for his.

Tempest felt the kiss in her dreams. Her lashes fluttered gently, then her eyes opened. She stared into the darkness of Stryker's eyes, finding, finally, the emotion that had been locked away since those moments of decision in his study. She started to lift her arms, to hold him. He caught her, holding her still.

"No. Give yourself to me, tonight, completely. Everything."

The words came as softly as each kiss that followed every syllable. As the kisses, they slipped into her mind, wrapping around her emotions until she had no choice but to agree. "Yes."

"No holding back."

"No. I belong to you." It was easy to say, although never thought before. She let the tension flow from her arms and left them on the bed beside her. She looked deeply into his eyes, sensing his need, echoing it. "Anything you want."

His smile was almost frightening with its sudden intensity as he lowered his head to her breast, his mouth open to take the taut peak. She moaned at the light scrape of his teeth on one, then the other. He caressed her stomach, feather-light touches that made her muscles quiver with sensation, her body undulate against his. It was torture, this slow hand he used. Sweet, unrelenting torture. Every inch of skin learned the heat of his kiss, the drugging dance of his fingers as they played with her nerve endings, her pulse points. She felt as though he were unraveling the very fabric of her being and then re-creating it in his own design. Her gasps of pleasure, surprised passion out of controlled desire, were the rhythm and the melody of the pas de deux. And when finally he rose above her, she watched him through eyes so heavy that it took all her strength to keep them open. He entered her slowly, by tiny degrees that sent her hurtling over the knife edge of pleasure on which he had kept her poised for so long. Her lashes fell, her cry of intense fulfillment was a lone sound in the silence, and still he kept filling her, stretching her until she was so completely mated with him that his breath and hers rose in unison.

"Now it begins," he whispered, brushing the tangled, damp hair back from her face.

Every muscle in his great body screamed for the release he wouldn't grant. This was his woman and it was time they both understood her commitment to him. His hips flexed, driving up so smoothly that Tempest felt the joining with every nerve. Her eyes opened but no sound passed her lips. She was floating, no strength to save herself, knowing no anchor but his power and the body that surged as gently and as relentlessly against hers as the evening tide. She moved with him, following, obeying his whispered instructions. Moisture beaded on her brow. Her skin glistened in the lamp light, gilded by his desire and her own. Tension coiled within as he rocked her, his hands sliding between them, touching her so that she called his name in a rush of panic and shock. She arched powerfully. Stryker controlled her easily, shifting her, deepening impossibly their union. His face was rigid with the demands he was forcing on his body. He knew he couldn't hold this peak of pleasure for longer than his next breath. But even he was unprepared for the sudden acceleration in passion. His control slipped, caught in the storm of his own creating. He wrapped his arms around Tempest, needing her as much as she needed him, his name called in the shadows by her voice, her name his answer as he took them to the white-hot fire that waited to brand them one. There was no tomorrow in that instant, No today. No future. No past. Just now. He slumped against her, spent, his breathing ragged, broken.

Tempest hardly had the strength to lift her arms, but she managed to cradle him against her as sleep stole her last conscious thought. She didn't know what had happened and in the morning there wouldn't be time to analyze the night. She would go, swiftly, cleanly, leaving behind questions that neither of them could answer.

THIRTEEN

Stryker stared at the fire as he sipped his brandy. One week since that night. One week of brief phone calls, emptiness, and worry. The team would begin the trip downriver tomorrow. His fingers tightened on the glass he held. Dan, the leader, had taken every precaution just as he had known he would. Tempest wouldn't even be in the first group going down. Thank God for small favors. She was still miffed about that decision. He smiled a little, thinking of her scarcely contained anger when she had told him about her friend's choices for the first party. He wondered if she had been furious enough to repeat to Dan the same aspersions on his ancestry and intelligence that she had muttered to Stryker.

As quickly as his amusement arrived, it left, his features once more resuming the worried cast that had come the moment her plane had lifted into the blue sky to carry her away from him. Even now he

wasn't certain he had done the right thing in sending
her to Indonesia alone. As for the night before she
left, it haunted him in ways he couldn't have imagined. He had thought to brand her but it was he who
wore her mark. No woman would ever please him
as she had done that night. No passion would ever
score him as deeply; no love would ever burn as
bright. But the sands of his allotted time with her
were trickling away more rapidly than he could
know. He couldn't shake the feeling that something
terrible would happen on that river. He had recognized the traces of his fear, at first, putting his
thoughts down to his usual response to any of her
dangerous undertakings. Now he felt it was more.
He raised his brandy to his lips, taking a large swallow of the vintage fire that did nothing to warm the
cold she had left behind.

"Choices. I made mine. You made yours. And
these are just the first. And God forgive me, maybe
the last." He finished the rest of his drink and poured
himself another from the carafe on the table beside
the chair. "May we both survive our decisions."

Tempest stared at the river, the lazy-looking
stretch that was their starting point. Two men of their
six-person group had started downriver this morning.
Watchers stationed in different places on the shore,
not many, for the area was not always accessible,
reported the first few rapids had caused no trouble.
The really tough white water wasn't due until
tomorrow.

"Getting antsy?" Dan asked, dropping a compan-
ionable arm over Tempest's shoulders.

"You know I am." She glared at him. "I still don't see why I have to be in the last group."

"We drew straws, remember."

"I think it was rigged."

"My partner said the same thing when that stomach virus made him yield his place to the alternate." He laughed, patting her shoulder. "I ended up in the second group. Think of the tips you'll get from the rest of us. It isn't likely that all of us will make it down without some land time. The last group will have the best chance. There are at least two stretches of water that are a witches' brew of trouble. And those falls are no picnic." He glanced over his shoulder to his partner. "Ready, partner?"

The other boater nodded before slipping into his craft.

"Cheer up, kid. I have only a few hours' start on you."

She grimaced, then relented. "Shut up and get on the river before I sabotage your boat and go in your place," she replied, going to hold his craft for him while he got in. As he pushed away from shore, she added, "Make sure you get down all right. I don't want to rescue your tail."

His laugh drifted over the deceptively calm water as he allowed the current to catch hold of his boat.

Tempest turned her attention to her own equipment. The groups were pushing off in timed intervals so that no potentially hazardous bottlenecks would occur. They had set up some radio communication on shore so that information between the three parties could be maintained. The arrangement was sketchy but it was better than no communication at all. The time lapse passed slowly and her nerves tightened in readiness for the demands she would soon make. She allowed her thoughts to drift to Stryker, remembering their last night, wishing she didn't feel as though he had been, somehow, saying good-bye. She paced the water's edge while her partner lay in the shade dozing. No matter how she tried to argue her image away, she still came back to feeling the elements of a farewell in the way he had held her, taking every ounce of passion as though it would be his last on this earth. The knowledge was shattering, frightening her as nothing had ever done. She stared at the river, thinking of the chances she had taken and won. Was this her last one? Foolish ideas that could cost her the edge she needed for survival. Yet, in spite of her well-honed ability to control her thoughts, her doubts, her fears, channeling them into skill, courage, and steel-rimmed nerves, she couldn't fight the memory of that night and the way she had felt as she had given herself to him as she had never done. Was life with that kind of passion, that capacity for giving, for creating worth the odds to which she had reduced it? Had she, in her need to fight the cage her family had tried to imprison her in, chosen to risk death rather than to build life?

"It's time, Tempest." Her partner joined her at the river's edge. "Ready?"

Tempest turned from her doubts, her questions, looking at her kayak. Only the light craft and her skill stood between her and the furious river. "Yes."

The phone rang in the silence of late evening, a startling sound that roused Stryker from his contemplation of the contract before him. He answered with half his attention. The unknown voice on the other end of the line brought his head up with a jerk.

"What did you say?" he demanded harshly, every bit of color fading from his skin, leaving his tan sallow with shock.

"I asked, Mr. McGuire, if you have been notified of your wife's accident yet?"

"What accident? Who the hell are you?" Stryker demanded, leaning forward, his whole body visibly rejecting the idea that Tempest had been hurt and he didn't know. Today should be the last leg of the trip. The worst of the water should even be over by now, given the time difference.

The man sighed audibly. "Three hours ago, the only woman on the trip was injured coming out of the last force-six rapid. They're bringing her in now, but the word is that she hasn't regained consciousness yet and that she's broken her back in at least one place."

Stryker's hand tightened on the receiver to the point of pain. "Who are you?" His voice was hoarse with fear that he didn't try to disguise.

"A reporter. A reputable one, I assure you. I'm not after a tabloid smear. I know your wife and a number of the team as a matter of fact. I had a couple of locals on the bank. They got word to me here in the city. The team hasn't made it out yet. Believe it or not, I thought you should know."

Stryker released his breath in a heavy sigh. "Are you sure it's her?"

"Temp . . . Mrs. McGuire was the only woman

on the main team. And a woman was injured. That's all I know for sure.''

"Your name?" Stryker flipped through his cardfile as he spoke.

"Raymond Knowles."

"I'm getting the first flight out. Call me through this number if you get anything else."

"Okay."

"I won't forget, Knowles."

"I didn't think you would," the man replied.

Stryker broke the connection and dialed the airfield where Arthur kept his private jet and gave his instructions to the ground crew with the proviso that Arthur would be calling shortly to confirm.

A few minutes later, his arrangements made, he rose and strode swiftly through the house, up the stairs to the room they shared. He threw some clothes at the case that habit had made him leave in the closet rather than store. He'd call Arthur on the way to the airport. Beyond that he didn't allow himself to think. Every action, every bit of mental energy was focused on reaching Tempest in the shortest possible time. He'd worry about her injuries, those who mattered to her, after he had her close. No matter what, he would move the universe to ensure that she survived. Life irreparably damaged was better than no life at all. He could live with possibility, hating it for her sake but so impossibly glad she had been spared one more time.

He stalked down the stairs, his case in hand, stopping suddenly on hearing the arrival of a car he didn't recognize. If those damn reporters had already gotten wind of Tempest's accident, he'd send them away with a blistering denial. Cursing, he snatched open the door, then stopped, frozen in place as he stared at the cab and the slender figure paying the fare.

When she turned and the light from the porch fell on her face, his muscles unknotted. Stryker went down the steps two at a time and hauled Tempest into his arms, locking her against his chest before she could finish saying his name. His mouth found hers, every ounce of relief and love pouring into his kiss. He didn't hear the cab driver's shocked admiration for his tactics or see the man finally leave.

Tempest strained against his hold, trying to squirm closer, needing him every bit as much as he needed her. Her hands speared into his hair as she fed on his mouth. "Never again," she whispered brokenly, tears raining down her face. "I will never fly again unless you fly with me." She looked into his eyes and saw the hell he had been suffering for her sake. She had never seen him so vulnerable or so beautiful. She had never felt more complete, more sure of herself than she did in this moment.

Stryker framed her features with hands that shook, drinking in the sight of her as a man thirsting in the desert. There would be time for questions later. All that mattered was that she was whole and with him. Then suddenly, her words filtered through his relief, his desperation to reach her. A nova of hope he hadn't dared to believe in exploded and his words came out in a disbelieving rush. "You mean that?"

Tempest read the shock, ached for him in ways she hadn't known possible. The magnitude of the love she had almost torn and stretched beyond fair limits stunned her silence for an instant. Humbled, awed by the strength of her man, his faith in her, his trust, she caught his wrists, holding him as he imprisoned her in the cage of his warm palms. "More than I mean anything, except I love you. I was a selfish, stupid fool. But no more. I don't need an adrenaline rush to define my life. All that proves is that I am flirting with death. You are my lover, my life. I need no substitute. No mountain I climb will ever be more challenging than my days with you. No risk I take and win will ever offer me more reward than I have found in your arms. No success I will ever have will have meaning when measured against the cost to both of us for what I steal to satisfy a whim and a dream born in the mind of a child-woman who needed to be loved.''

Tears flowed without end down her face and she let him see her weakness, his power over her. There was no more to fear. Stryker would never use her love as a chain to bring her to heel. She was finally, totally free to be the woman she was meant to be, his wife, his mate, his lover, his woman. "You love me. I was fool enough to need proof. You were strong enough to give it to me in letting me go. I didn't recognize your gift for what it was until the end of that first day on the river. I slid into rapids churning with nature's fury. I fought my way out to calm water again and I felt nothing. No exhilaration, no pride, no need to push on, to grab for more. I sat in that boat, staring at the sky, the silence of the land waiting for me to be fool enough to try to conquer it, learning as it has always known that, no matter what, Nature would always be the ultimate winner. My triumph would always lie in the dust that would mark the end of my existence.'' She smiled softly through the tears, her eyes serene, her belief in herself and the future they would build together perfect. She was at peace and it showed like a candle held aloft in the dead of night.

''You are my life. That simple. No regrets. No needs. No wishes for more than I hold right now.''

Stryker traced the path of her tears, the peace that lay in her eyes as she looked at him. Perhaps, the heaven he held in his hands was measured by the depths of the hell he had survived. He didn't know. It wouldn't have mattered had he been certain. He would have lived these days and nights again and all the ones that had gone before for this one instant.

''I love you.'' He touched her smile, then matched it with his own in his kiss. ''I'm glad you're home.'' He lifted her in his arms and carried her up the front steps into the home they had made together. Her hands caressed his face with a gentleness, a tenderness that would always be in her touch for him. His eyes never left hers as he bore her up the stairs to their room and the waiting darkness that would always be there, their haven against the world.

''I love you more than my life.'' His whisper was a vow.

''I give you mine with that same love for all time.'' Her reply was a promise that would never be broken.